The
Feast
of the
Drowned

BY STEPHEN COLE

BBC
BOOKS

10 8 6 4 2 1 3 5 7 9

BBC Books, an imprint of Ebury Publishing
20 Vauxhall Bridge Road,
London SW1V 2SA

BBC Books is part of the Penguin Random House group of companies
whose addresses can be found at global.penguinrandomhouse.com

Penguin
Random House
UK

Executive producers: Steven Moffat and Brian Minchin

First published by BBC Books in 2006

www.eburypublishing.co.uk

A CIP catalogue record for this book is
available from the British Library

ISBN 9781785940507

Commissioning Editor: Stuart Cooper
Creative Director and Editor: Justin Richards
Consultant Editor: Helen Raynor
Production Controller: Alenka Oblak

Cover design by Henry Steadman © BBC 2006
Typeset in Albertina by Rocket Editorial, Aylesbury, Bucks
Printed and bound in Great Britain by Clays Ltd, St Ives PLC

DOCTOR·WHO

The Feast of the Drowned

04367785

For Paul Magrs

How can something so big sink so fast? The thought kept drumming through Jay Selby's head. He splashed and slithered over the slippery deck. It listed so sharply to starboard he could barely keep his footing.

The wind whipped at his uniform, stung his skin. He stared around as if he might sight the enemy. Nothing. The black sky, the churning darkness of the North Sea, there was no difference between them.

'No lifeboats!' The shouts rose above the roar of the sea. 'They've taken the lifeboats!'

There was a crew of 173 on board HMS *Ascendant*, tough, capable sailors all of them. *They shouldn't be screaming,* Jay thought. He clung on to a rail as a crowd of ratings scrambled past him. *They shouldn't be screaming. We shouldn't be sinking so damned fast.*

The frigate was armed to the teeth: Sea Wolf missiles, torpedoes, the Vickers gun. She could clobber anything from a submarine to an enemy fighter, so why were they sinking without a single shot fired?

One of the ratings slipped and fell. Jay staggered over, helped him up. It was Barker, the loudmouth, the blond joker; part of the gun crew. He looked terrified.

'We've got to get to the upper deck,' Barker shouted. 'They took –'

'The lifeboats, I know.' Jay dragged him to his feet. 'But *what* took them?'

Barker gripped hold of Jay's arm, shaking with cold and shock. 'Sonar didn't show 'em. Like they came out of nowhere.'

Jay pulled himself free, slipped an arm around Barker's shoulder. 'Upper deck, then,' he shouted. 'Come on. The Lynx must have got clear, it'll be circling. They'll radio our –'

'You didn't see?'

'I was in the stores, didn't see nothing.'

'The chopper's gone.' Barker stared at him, pale in the weak glow of the frigate's failing lights. 'The whole aft section…'

Then the deck lurched again with incredible force. As if launched from a cannon, they crashed into the black mirror of the sea. It was hard as glass, smashed the air from him. Jay clutched hold of Barker as they dropped down through the freezing water. He couldn't see a thing but he knew he had to keep calm, reach the surface. His limbs felt so heavy but he started to kick, to push himself up. Something rushed past him, going down. Wreckage? One of the crew?

What?

Lungs bursting, pressure swarming at his temples, Jay kept on kicking. His fingers were numb, hooked into Barker's uniform. *Don't let go. It's OK. You can do this.* Wasn't that what

Keisha always used to say? *You can do this*. Whenever he messed up, whenever he just wanted out, she took hold of his arms just like Jay had hold of Barker now and told him.

He thought of her back home. They were meant to be meeting up in just a couple of weeks. He was going to cook her steaks – juicy, fat, fillet steaks, the kind they had used to dream about, the melt-in-the-mouth sort Mum could never afford. 'Cause he was doing all right now, and he wanted to show her that. Mum had never believed in a damn thing he did, but Keisha…

Jay thought of her face, of the hurt in her eyes when he'd left.

He kicked harder. *I can do this.*

Then Barker's body was wrenched away from him.

Jay gasped. Water jumped in like an icy fist down his throat. He choked, floundered. *Don't lose it. Don't lose it.* His chest felt crushed, his limbs were cramping. But he had to go back for Barker. What had pulled him away – sharks?

Thrashing in the water, Jay finally broke back through the surface. Choking on icy air, spitting out saltwater, throat burning. Skin numb, no sensation, as if it had died ahead of him.

He stared round. No sign of his ship, or Barker. No sign of anyone. Only him, floating alone in endless shadow.

For a long, eerie moment he felt almost calm, lulled by the wash of the sea as it shifted all around him.

Then something closed around his ankle and plucked him back beneath the waves.

Jay windmilled his arms, tried to kick free. One of his

crewmates, panicking, grabbing hold of anything in the water?

Something rushed through the water again, close by. Something that slammed into his back and punctured the skin at the base of his neck. Jay felt sudden heat and pain. Wanted to open his mouth and scream. It wasn't black down here any more, there was a red, warning glow coming from somewhere. Like he was being dragged slowly down into hell.

I can't do this, Keisha. He could see horrible shapes twisting and spiralling in slow-mo through the gloom. Cartwheeling corpses. Chunks of metal and equipment, juggled by unseen hands. Other things, too. Swift, hunting things. Creatures.

Was it one of those gnawing now at the back of his neck, as hungrily as he and Keisha would take those steaks? He breathed in water, wanted the blackness back.

But Jay could see everything now, and the cold dead eyes of the hunting creatures might just as well have been his own.

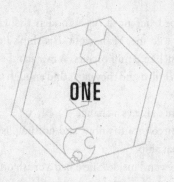

ONE

'I'm so sorry, Keish.' Rose Tyler sat on the threadbare sofa and held her old mate close. She couldn't think of anything to say that didn't sound useless and hollow, but she kept trying. 'I'm really, really sorry. When Mum told me, I just... Well, it's so hard to take in.'

Keisha sniffed noisily and pulled away. She was one of Rose's old clubbing crowd, wildest and loudest and craziest of the lot. She looked totally gorgeous when she was glammed up. But right now her black curls were ratted and her light brown skin was snail-trailed with snot and tears. 'Jay was my brother,' she murmured. 'And now he's just gone.'

There was a picture of him on the cheap Ikea sideboard – a big, grinning, burly boy. The chipped, imitation pine looked too thin to support such a warm and healthy figure.

'Have they told your mum? The navy, I mean.'

'Doubt it. Got no address for her, no phone number... She wouldn't care anyway. Got her other family now.'

'Yeah, but she still... I mean, she *must*...' Again, Rose found herself trailing off. This wasn't helping.

Keisha wiped her nose on a sodden tissue. "'Missing in action," they told me. Yeah, right. His ship's been towed up the Thames in, like, a million bits. Why can't they just own up that he's been killed and they can't find enough of him to send back home?'

'Keish, there's always a chance –'

'It's been three months now, and nothing. Nothing left of anyone on that ship.'

Rose felt so weird inside. She'd had a crush on Jay when she was fourteen. That was five years ago and, daft though it was, she'd never really been able to talk to him properly since. Now she never would, and it didn't seem real.

So much had happened in her own life since then… She'd seen so much death in so many far-flung times and places, she was sort of hardened to it. Now someone from her old life here in London was never coming back, and Keisha was showing her the repercussions up close and personal. Rose found she had no idea how to relate to it.

The Doctor was being no help at all of course. He just stood there, staring out of the window. She wasn't sure if he was sulking 'cause she'd dragged him along here today, or if he was actually just enjoying the grey concrete view of the surrounding high-rises from here on the third floor. Who could tell? She'd known him for ages now, but still she couldn't always read his moods.

'Who's your mate?' Keisha whispered, wiping her nose.

Rose shut her eyes. *A 900-year-old alien, actually. He lives in a police box that's really a spaceship called the TARDIS and we fight monsters and save planets. It's brilliant, you should try it. Maybe not,* she decided. 'He's just the Doctor.'

Keisha shot her a suspicious look. 'I don't need a doctor.'

'Not *that* sort of doctor, Keish, he's… Well, he's…' Rose floundered, looked over at him in his brown pinstripe suit and grubby sneakers, hoping for inspiration. 'He's sort of like those disk doctors down the big PC shops. Good with computers and that.'

'Oh.' Keisha nodded, apparently satisfied. 'You met him when you went away that time, yeah?'

'Kind of.'

'Suppose you must have met all sorts, living abroad for a year… while your poor old mates left behind were worried sick.' Rose caught the disapproval behind the smile. 'We thought that loser Mickey had topped you or something.'

'Long time ago now.' Rose hid behind a rueful smile, cringing inside. When she'd first gone off into space and time, the Doctor claimed he could bring her back to Earth the day after she'd left. But he'd messed up. They'd come back a whole twelve months later.

'You could have told us you were going.' Keisha nudged her. 'Better yet, could have taken us with you! And you've been back in the country for months and months, ain't you? Where've you been? It ain't been the same round here without you, babes. I've really missed you.'

'It's good to see you too,' Rose said. 'I'm just sorry it took… something like this to put my bum in gear and make me get my act together.'

"S'all right. Nothing really lasts, does it?' Keisha shrugged, staring into space again. 'Friendships… family…'

Rose shook her head. 'Hey, come on, Keish. Look, I'm gonna be around for a few days –'

'A few days!' The Doctor snapped into life, whirled round, gave her a look as sharp as his angular features. Then he realised Keisha was watching him and his face softened. He started nodding. 'Yeah. A few days, course we are. Thought so.' When Keisha looked away he grimaced and mouthed at Rose, 'A few *days*?'

Rose gave him an *and your problem is…?* look back, then squeezed Keisha's hand. 'So anyway, I'll be around. A proper mate. We can do stuff – go out, or… maybe just stay in, yeah? Watch videos or something.'

'What did Jay do in the navy?' the Doctor asked abruptly.

Keisha blinked. 'He did something in the ship's stores. Spare parts and stuff.'

'Naval Stores Sub Department.' The Doctor wore a proper boy's smile. 'Oh, that's a brilliant job. There are 42,000 spare parts on your average frigate – think what you could make with that lot! And they call those stores assistants Jack Dusties, don't they? Why is that?' The smile became a crooked grin. 'Imagine if your name was Jack Dusty and you became a Jack Dusty! And then if Jack Dusty the Jack Dusty went to the planet Jacdusta in the Dustijek nebula and joined *their* navy, he could…'

Keisha was staring at him as if he had two heads. Rose had turned her *pack it in* glare up to 11 and he finally noticed.

'Chips,' the Doctor said suddenly. 'Chips would be good now. Who wants chips?'

'Sounds great,' said Rose quickly. She pressed a fiver into

his hand, in case he tried to pay with a twenty-zarg note or something. 'The Chinese round the corner does them good and greasy.'

'In foil trays, I suppose?' The Doctor looked suddenly crestfallen. 'You know, chips have never tasted the same since they stopped wrapping them in newspaper. I liked them in newspaper.'

'Well, there's a newsagent's next door. Buy a paper with the change on your way back!'

He perked up. 'Good thinking. Yeah, nice one. OK! Back in a minute.'

He picked his way through the clutter in the poky flat to the front door and slammed it closed behind him.

Rose could relax at last. 'Sorry. Sometimes he gets a bit…'

'Fruit-loops?'

'Hyper.'

Keisha nodded. 'He's cute, anyway. Not really like your mum described, though.'

Rose smiled to herself. 'You could say he's pretty indescribable, yeah.'

They sat in silence for a while, the atmosphere lightened a little by the Doctor's odd outburst.

And then a ghost appeared in the corner of the room.

Rose stared dumbly, her skin puckering with goosebumps. Keisha gripped hold of Rose's arm, dug her nails in tight.

It was Jay. He was standing between them and the turned-off telly, a terrified, translucent phantom, soaked and shivering.

'D'you see him, Rose?' Keisha whispered, starting to shake.

'Am I crazy, or –'

'No, I see him,' Rose croaked, rooted to the spot. 'I see *something*, anyway.'

'Then he's not dead! He – he's all right!'

Rose didn't answer as she gently prised Keisha's fingers free. Whatever was standing in front of them was a long way from being all right.

'Help me, Keish.' Jay's ghostly voice was muted and faint, and his lips didn't move in time with the words. 'Help me.'

Keisha swallowed. 'Jay? Jay… What is it, babes?'

'Come to me,' the phantom whispered.

'Come?' She shook her head, fresh tears falling. 'I – What d'you mean?'

'Come to me.'

'Where are you?'

'You gotta come to me,' Jay said. 'Before the feast.'

'Feast?' Rose summoned her courage and got up unsteadily. 'Jay, if that's you –'

Jay turned to look straight at her. 'Little Rose Tyler.' She felt a shiver graze her spine as a smile crept on to his face, as his image grew a little brighter, a little more solid. 'You gotta come too.' He took a silent step towards them. 'Please.'

Trembling, Rose sat straight back down on the bed. 'Come where? I don't –'

'You've got to get to me before the feast.'

He was growing fainter.

'Jay!' Keisha shook her head. 'Stay with me, babes. Don't go.'

Then, as Rose stared in horror, Jay's features began to run, like a chalk drawing left out in the rain. His uniform too, it was dripping away. His jaw dropped open and Keisha screamed as water gushed out from his mouth.

Then the image was gone. All that was left was a large pooling puddle on the carpet in front of the telly. Then that seemed to soak away, leaving nothing behind.

Rose started as Keisha's icy fingers grabbed at her hand. 'Gone,' she breathed. 'Was that really him? Was that Jay?'

'I dunno.' Rose squeezed her friend's frozen hand.

'That *was* him,' Keisha decided, wiping her eyes with her free hand. 'Why was I so scared? It was *him*, Rose! He needs me!'

'Me and all, apparently,' Rose reminded her, still reeling. 'But what's all this about a –'

'Feast your eyes!' cried the Doctor, bursting into the room with a steaming white plastic bag. Rose gasped and Keisha almost jumped a mile. 'Hot, salty chips. Foil trays, no papers I'm afraid – newsagent's is shut, full of fainting customers. Maybe it's his prices, what d'you reckon? Anyway, ambulance is on the way so I didn't hang around. Where are the plates? Nothing worse than cold chips…'

'Doctor,' Rose began shakily.

Finally he seemed to take in that something was wrong and his features sharpened in alarm. 'You all right?'

'No!' She shook her head. 'I – we saw – that is… I think we just…'

Keisha was quite calm, her eyes shining as she stared into space. 'Jay came back.'

The Doctor blinked. 'What?'

Rose nodded. 'He did. We saw him.'

'This could be serious,' said the Doctor gravely, dropping the plastic bag. 'I only got enough chips for three.'

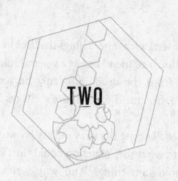

TWO

Rose went a step or two ahead of the Doctor through the concrete walkways of the estate. Keisha had asked them both to leave, said she was tired out, and Rose could hardly insist they stayed. But she wasn't sure Keisha should be left alone, especially after what they'd witnessed.

'I'll come back later on, yeah?' She'd lingered in the doorway, uneasy. 'You hope *he's* gonna come back, don't you?'

'He's my brother,' said Keisha simply.

Out here in the pale sunlight Rose found it hard to believe how scared she had been; hard to believe it had happened at all. Now she and the Doctor were on their way back to her mum's. She could sense how eager he was to get going, to escape this world and the remnants of her old life, to remind her of how fantastic her new life with him could be.

But Rose wasn't ready to move on again just yet. When they reached the garages, she stopped walking. 'What do *you* think we saw?'

The Doctor carried on for several paces before he realised she was no longer beside him. 'I don't know.'

'A ghost?'

'I've never seen a real one. Things that *look* like ghosts, yeah – loads and loads of them. But as a general rule people never come back from the dead.' Suddenly he sounded almost bitter, like a frustrated kid. 'There's always been another explanation.'

Rose sighed. 'I s'pose the navy did say Jay was only missing in action. But what sort of action could turn him into a… a whooshy hologram thing? And why wait three months before coming to haunt his sister?'

'Maybe he followed his ship home. Keisha said it had been towed up the Thames, didn't she?' He pulled a face. 'Why bother, though? Why bring it into the middle of London?' Then he spun round and tried to set off again.

'Oi!' Rose pulled on his arm, stopped him. 'I know you're dying to get off… But can we try to find out first?'

'Course we can. First stop, Mickey's place. We need to find out more about the *Ascendant* – where it sank, what's happened to it since then, see if anything fishy's been going on. Quick dolphin-friendly trawl through the Internet should do it. Then we'll take it from there.'

'Wow,' said Rose, batting her eyelids at him. 'I never knew – my wish really is your command.'

The Doctor grinned. 'One bag of chips and I'm anyone's.'

'Ten-foot green aliens, I can handle. Warrior monsters in dirty great spaceships, I'm your man. But ghosts?' Mickey Smith grinned, shook his head. 'You're winding me up.'

Rose scowled. Usually she loved Mickey's smile. It was one

of the first things that had attracted her to him – that and his smooth dark skin, his playful eyes, his easygoing outlook on life. But right now he was bugging her big-time.

'I said he *looked* like a ghost. Don't you believe me?'

'I'm your ex, not your exorcist.'

He said it lightly but there was an edge to his words. They'd been going out before she'd gone off with the Doctor. Now they were still close, but in a different way. More like friends. Kind of.

Sometimes it did Rose's head in.

She looked past Mickey at the Doctor, who was on the computer in the untidy bedroom. He was staring intently at the screen, hammering the keys and slamming down on the mouse, tutting and cursing under his breath. 'This is so slow!'

'Oi, don't break it,' Mickey told him. 'What are you looking up, anyway?'

'Anything on that ship, the HMS *Ascendant*.'

'Oh, that. You should've said.' Mickey stroked his chin, playing the great thinker. 'Type twenty-three, 430 feet long and weighing almost 5,000 tons. Stealth design. They can operate anywhere in the world.'

'They can sink anywhere in the world too, by the looks of it.'

Rose looked at Mickey suspiciously. 'How come you know so much about it?'

'I'm a boy. It's genetic.' He picked up some printouts from beneath a bundle of clothes on the floor and tossed them over to the Doctor. 'And 'cause I did some research on that boat when it got tugged up the Thames. Thought it sounded a bit sus.' He looked pointedly at Rose. 'It's what I do now. Dig around and find stuff you might want to know about next time you drop in.'

'Nice one, Mickey.' The Doctor slapped him on the back. 'Who says you're a total waste of space with no life?'

'You do.'

'And I'm right too, aren't I? You really need to get out more.' He riffled through the papers. 'Hmm, sank just over three months ago... all hands lost, big tragedy... Full government inquiry, blah blah blah...'

'Ninety million quid, that ship cost. Now it's just scrap.' Mickey shook his head. 'They're bound to want to find out what happened.'

Rose shrugged. 'Won't bring back the sailors, will it?'

'Maybe it already has,' said Mickey. 'If this Jay bloke really did show up.'

'Keisha saw him too!' said Rose hotly.

Mickey folded his arms. 'Yeah? Doesn't say much, does it?'

'Oh, right, now I get it. This is about Keisha, right? Any other time you'd *say* you believed me even if you didn't, just to shut me up. But because it's her we're talking about, you don't want to know.'

'That's not true!'

The Doctor nipped in between them, waved a printout under Rose's nose. 'Hooray! Look. Stanchion House. Government-owned marine engineering plant on the bank of the Thames, near Southwark. Now we know where the ship's been taken. That's good. Bunting alert! Isn't that good?'

'Great.' Rose crossly snatched the paper and glanced at it. 'I know you never liked Keisha, Mickey. "Oooh, ditch her, babe, she's a bad influence –'"

'She is!' He shook his head. 'The state of you after a night out with her!'

'Oh, and I was so much worse than you coming back from your stupid lads' get-togethers…' Rose tailed off. 'Pieces.'

'What?'

'Why did they bring Jay's ship back in pieces?'

'I dunno…' Mickey shrugged, suddenly wrong-footed. 'It's been three months. Maybe they dismantled it, ready to send different bits to different departments at this Stanchion House place.'

'Good theory.' The Doctor shoved the papers back into Mickey's hands. 'Why?'

'So they can study all the different bits quicker, maybe?'

The Doctor picked up a newspaper from the desk. 'No, I mean, why was Keisha a bad influence?'

'She wasn't,' said Rose flatly.

'Oh yeah, right,' said Mickey. 'I've heard about some of those dives she dragged you to. And about the blokes who go there.'

'That's not fair.'

'Was it fair when she got her mates to push things through my letter box?' he said more quietly. 'Or when she tried to have them beat a confession out of me?'

'What are you on about?'

Mickey nodded across to the Doctor. 'When you went off in the TARDIS with *him* for a year. And your mum told everyone I'd done away with you.'

'So I was a bit out with the timing!' The Doctor mimed a pantomime yawn and slumped in a chair. 'I've said I was sorry.'

'Yeah. Which is more than Keisha ever did.'

'I didn't know she'd done those things,' Rose conceded.

Mickey shrugged. 'Well, you ain't had too much time for your old life lately, have you?'

'Old life, new life, they're all the same!' The Doctor jumped back up, threw an arm round each of them, then froze. He moved his jaw awkwardly. 'Except the teeth. It can be weird getting used to the teeth. Now, kiss and make up, because this is *very* interesting.' The Doctor tapped the newspaper. 'It says here that as many as twenty people have gone missing near that part of the Thames since the *Ascendant* turned up.'

'I know,' said Mickey. '"Curse of the Ghost Ship", they call it… Probably made it up to cash in and sell more copies.' He paused. 'Didn't they?'

'I reckon it's time we had a look at what's left of this ship for ourselves,' the Doctor declared, grinning away. 'Who's coming? We can take the TARDIS. Have you back here, oooh, thirty seconds after we left. Deal? Who's in? Come on, who's in?'

Rose and Mickey looked at each other. She spoke for them both.

'All right, we're coming. But we're all taking the bus.'

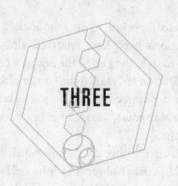

THREE

'Well, where can that ship have got to?' said Rose dryly, staring out over the Thames in the evening sunlight. Uniformed men stood stiffly on the deck of a squat, powerful tug. A huge, blocky shape was moored behind it, shrouded in tarpaulins. Both stood close to a white-stone three-storey building: Stanchion House, as grand and anonymous as any other old building lurking along this stretch of river. Only the tell-tale signs of the marines flanking the great glass doorway gave away its significance.

'How are we supposed to see what's left of the ship with that lot around?' Mickey wondered.

'First we've got to get across,' said Rose. 'And the nearest bridges have all been closed off to the public.'

'Hasn't stopped her.' The Doctor pointed to a nearby suspension bridge, spoiled by scaffolding and graffiti. An old woman, smartly dressed in green, stood close to the side, staring out at the ship.

Suddenly, she started to climb up over the iron mesh of the safety rail.

Mickey stared, appalled. 'What's she doing?'

'What's it look like?' Rose muttered, already haring off towards the steps leading up to the bridge, a couple of paces behind the Doctor. He vaulted the barrier blocking the way and took the steps three at a time, his suit jacket flapping as if in its own private panic. Rose felt her heart pounding as she raced after him.

'Omigod,' she breathed as they rounded the top of the steps. The old woman had very nearly hauled herself up on to the side of the bridge. She'd have been over the edge by now if not for her long, tweedy skirt slowing her down. No one else was in sight. 'She's gonna do it! Chuck herself in!'

The Doctor skidded to a stop. 'Excuse me!' he called cheerily. 'Um, I'm looking for Piccadilly Circus. Am I lost?'

'He needs me,' said the woman without turning.

'Who, me? I do! I certainly do, you're right there.' The Doctor slowly crept towards her. 'I could be wandering around bridges and stuff all night if you don't come down and give me a hand.'

'Why don't we help you down,' said Rose, 'so you can show him the way?'

'He needs me to get to him,' the old woman went on, 'before the feast.'

Rose's blood ran cold. 'That's what Jay said.'

The Doctor nodded. 'This person who needs you, love... was he on board the *Ascendant* when she went down?'

'I must help him,' the woman declared, straightening her skirt demurely as she balanced on the edge of the bridge. 'I thought he was lost, but now –'

'He's back. Yeah, you've seen him, haven't you?' the Doctor asked casually. 'Tell us about it. Tell us your name.'

'Anne.' She shook her head, the gentle breeze ruffling her white wavy hair. 'I can't help you. I'm not from round here.'

'Where *are* you from?'

'Edinburgh. I only came here because…' A sad smile. 'I don't much want to talk. No one would believe me anyway.'

'Try us!' Rose insisted, looking up at her. 'Because we've seen someone too. Someone else who served on the ship, Jay Selby. He was a… What was it?'

'A Jack Dusty,' said the Doctor, edging closer. 'Or was Jack Dusty a Jay Selby?' He looked at her intently. 'Which way round is it, Anne, can you tell me?'

The old woman smiled, turned back to face him. 'I was a Wren Dusty in the sixties. My husband was a surgeon lieutenant. We always wanted Peter to go into the navy. And he did so well for himself.'

'Peter, right!' The Doctor nodded encouragingly. 'I think Jay knew him. Yeah, course he did! Come down for a few minutes and tell us what Peter said.' The Doctor offered his hand to her. 'We won't keep you long. Thirty seconds. A minute, tops. Come on, that's it…'

Rose held her breath as slowly, painfully slowly, Anne reached out her own hand to take his.

'Look out!' shouted Mickey, who'd made it to the top of the bridge.

Anne looked up sharply, wavering for a second as if she was about to overbalance. The Doctor lunged for her hand, pulled her forwards. Rose tried to break the woman's fall by getting underneath her. All three went down in a heap.

'Mickey, have you gone nuts?' Rose cried.

'Maybe.' He was looking past them. 'But I reckon this lot are gonna *do* their nuts.'

Rose turned to see a wall of khaki sprinting towards them from the other end of the bridge. The asphalt floor rumbled with the boom of their boots. 'Soldiers. Great. Now we're for it.'

Anne was on her hands and knees, her tweed skirt stained with oil. There was this weird look on her face...

The soldiers clattered to a halt. 'You saw the blockade. This bridge is closed to the public,' snapped a lean, hard-faced girl, leader of the troop. 'It's open to Stanchion House personnel only. You've got no business to be here.'

'Don't give me that. We had to help this woman,' said the Doctor. 'You can see for yourself she's not right. Had a bit of a shock. You lot storming up here –'

'We'll arrange medical care. You must clear this...' The girl soldier frowned, put a hand to her head as if she was in pain. 'Clear this area.'

'Hey, are you all right?' said Rose. 'You don't look too...'

The soldier girl sank to her knees.

Anne's grazed, dirty hand flew to her mouth. 'Oh, my love...'

The soldiers started dropping to the ground, one by one.

'What's happening to them?' asked Rose, her voice rising in fear.

'Dunno. No idea. Some sort of seizure?' The Doctor quickly examined the girl soldier. 'Low blood pressure. Heart's beating like crazy...' He grabbed her flailing wrist and pinched the skin.

Rose stared at him. 'And that helps her how exactly?'

'Peter!' Anne shouted.

Mickey staggered backwards. 'God, I feel sick.'

'Get out of here, Mickey, back down the steps,' the Doctor ordered. 'Call an ambulance for this lot, double quick.'

He nodded, backed away. 'Got it.'

'Chop-chop,' the Doctor added, looking worriedly into Anne's eyes. 'Pronto. *Prontissimo.*'

'Are the soldiers bad?' asked Rose.

'Yes.' The Doctor turned to one of the other soldiers, pinched a fold of skin on his neck. 'Rose, get Anne out of here. Take her somewhere comfy she can rest. Look after her.'

'What about you?'

'These soldiers were guarding Stanchion House. Now they're sleeping on the job it'll be easier to get in, won't it? 'Specially with one of their pass cards.' He straightened up, showed her what looked like a white credit card, and gave her a wild grin. 'Golden opportunity! Got to grab it while I can.'

'But there'll be loads more guards inside!' Rose protested.

Anne shouted out, suddenly desperate. 'Peter, come back!'

The Doctor placed his hands on Rose's shoulders. 'Stay with her. Don't let her out of your sight.' Without another word, he legged it off down the deserted bridge.

'Mickey, hurry up with that ambulance!' Rose shouted, trying to gently pull Anne up into a standing position. 'Come on. Come with me. Peter will be back.' A shiver ran through her; she'd meant it to sound soothing but it came out more like a threat.

As she moved the old woman away, the soldiers stopped

twitching. Something like water pooled up from the asphalt and trickled over to the side of the bridge. Then, as if it had drained into the iron and paintwork, it was gone.

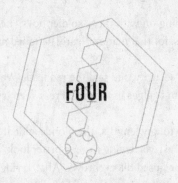

FOUR

The Doctor soon reached the dark glass doors of the imposing stone building. He checked his reflection, made a vague swipe at straightening his tie, then pushed inside.

He found himself in a posh foyer, all brightness and marble. A large, disgruntled-looking security guard eyed him from the back of the hall. The Doctor ignored him as he slotted his stolen pass card into a turnstile, which beeped politely and let him through.

Two girls manned the high-tech reception, a blonde and a redhead looking smart as paint in dark navy blue. 'May we help you?' asked the blonde.

The Doctor ambled over. *Be bold*, he decided. 'Sir John Smith, Scientific Adviser to the Admiralty, at your service.' He pulled out a battered leather wallet and waved it in front of them. 'I know I have an honest face, but here's my ID. Just so you're sure.'

Both girls nodded and smiled; the paper was low-level psychic, and showed them exactly what they expected to see. 'Who are you visiting, sir?'

'What's going on with those soldier boys?' he said quickly. 'And the girls, for that matter. Nearly flattened me on my way in here.'

'Just extra security, sir,' said the redhead. 'We've closed off the pedestrian bridges in the area. Press keep trying to sneak past.'

'They'll go to any lengths,' the blonde added. 'They're even jumping in the river, trying to get a better look.'

The Doctor raised his eyebrows. 'Aha! Trying to get to the *Ascendant*, are they? Or on the trail of all those people who've disappeared around here lately?'

The redhead shrugged awkwardly. 'You know how the press likes to blow these things up.'

'Ruddy cheek! Blowing things up is a job for the armed forces.' He smiled, glanced down at the visitors' book to see who had been called on already today. 'Anyway, I'm here to see, er, V. Swann.'

'Vida from Ocean Research.'

'Yep, that's her. Floor thingummy, isn't it?'

'Derek will take you,' said the redhead, nodding to the burly security guard.

'No need for that, I can find my own way. I've got clearance and everything.'

'And I operate the lift, sir,' said Derek firmly. He gestured to the large grey doors in the wall behind him, which swished open at the press of a button.

'Oh. Well, then.' The Doctor treated Derek to his very biggest grin. 'Take me to your Vida.'

* * *

Rose found it wasn't just Anne she had to look after. Mickey had been sick, and was now sat on the bottom step with his head between his legs.

'This feeling just came over me,' he moaned. 'My mouth went dry, I got all dizzy and then…'

'I think we all heard what happened next, thanks.' Rose grimaced, slipped her hooded top around Anne. The old woman had gone deathly quiet, staring out into space.

'Just so you know, I wasn't sick 'cause I was scared or nothing.'

'Don't be silly. I'm just glad what happened to the soldiers didn't happen to you.'

'You mean you'd actually care?'

She sighed. 'Don't milk it, Mickey.'

'Milk! If only. I'm dying of thirst.' He wiped his lips on the back of his hand. 'What about the old girl, then, she all right now?'

'Dunno. Anne? How're you doing?' No response. It was as if she'd retreated into herself. 'She needs rest. Somewhere clean and comfy.'

'Rules out my place,' said Mickey. 'What about your mum's?'

Rose nodded, glanced at her mobile. 'At least Anne's doing better than the soldiers. Hope that ambulance gets here in a minute.'

'An ambulance won't be necessary.'

The dry, dusty voice made Rose jump up. She turned to find that a spindly old man in full naval uniform had appeared behind them on the steps, flanked by two more soldiers. From all the braid and bling on his cap and blazer he was someone pretty important too. He wore dark glasses, and a thin white scarf was bundled about his neck.

'What d'you mean it won't be necessary?' Rose demanded. 'Didn't you see those soldiers up there? They had some sort of fit.'

'They will recover shortly,' the newcomer informed them, stalking down the steps towards them.

'Who are you, then?'

'Rear Admiral John Crayshaw.' He smiled faintly, cheerlessly. 'Now, I understand this woman tried to throw herself from the bridge.'

'She's all right now,' said Mickey, wincing as he tried to get up. 'We were just going.'

Crayshaw shook his head, the pink evening sun flashing off his dark glasses. 'I think perhaps I should look after her personally.'

Rose frowned. 'Why?'

'This area is out of bounds to members of the public.'

'Because so many members of the public have disappeared?' Mickey challenged. 'We've read the papers. We know something weird's going on, and it's linked to that ship.'

'I am managing a routine situation and everything is under control.' Crayshaw kept looking at Anne. 'Very well, you may go. Remove yourselves from this area.'

'We're going,' Rose assured him.

'And no plans to return?'

'What're you on about?'

He looked unsettlingly pleased with himself, but said

nothing. As if he was enjoying some secret joke.

Rose turned her back on him, moved off with Mickey as fast as Anne would allow. She heard his bone-dry voice barking orders as they left.

'You – wait for the ambulance and send it on its way. Guard this approach. If anyone tries to copy the old woman's antics, apprehend them and contact me at once. And you – with me.'

'Watch out, Doctor,' Rose murmured. 'Captain Bird's-Eye is on the warpath.'

The Doctor had been taken up to the third floor, and now Derek the doorman was leading him down a corridor. For a state-of-the-art engineering complex it was all surprisingly homely – patterned carpets, dashing naval figures in frames on the whitewashed walls, grand sash windows letting in plenty of light. Filing cabinets and busts on plinths jostled for space on either side of the walkway, which was barely wide enough to accommodate the guard's girth.

Not a sign of a workshop or a lab or a bit of old boat anywhere, reflected the Doctor glumly. He wasn't going to find much up here – besides a dubious welcome from Vida Swann.

'Her office is at the end on your right,' Derek announced. 'You'll need your pass.'

'Of course.' The Doctor produced his white card with a flourish and carried on down the corridor. 'Well, thanks for the guided tour. Bye.'

But Derek didn't shift, watching him with a hangdog expression.

The Doctor paused uncomfortably outside the office door. 'I'm here. Safe and sound.'

Derek nodded. 'In you go, sir.'

'Oh, yeah. Right.' He contemplated the white card for a few moments. Would those soldiers have access privileges for this level? If not, the next few minutes could be seriously embarrassing. 'Here we go, then!'

He rammed the white card home. With a quiet bleep and a click, the door jumped off its catch. With a triumphant wave at Derek, the Doctor disappeared inside.

The office was small; room for a desk and an internal door and not a lot else. On this second door, a piece of paper had been taped over an existing nameplate, and he stepped forward to read it. In block capitals was printed:

VIDA SWANN – LIAISON OFFICER

EUROPEAN OFFICE OF OCEANIC RESEARCH AND DEVELOPMENT

Then suddenly the door opened outwards and bashed him on the nose. 'Ow!'

'Whoops! Oh, God, I'm sorry!' A willowy blonde swept out from behind the heavy oak door and grasped his face with both hands. 'Are you all right? Are you bleeding?'

'I'm fine!' he protested.

'Shall I get you a tissue?'

'I don't need to blow it, thanks.' He pulled his face free of her grasp. 'Well. Hello, then. You're Vida Swann.'

'Yes, I am.' She looked around the antechamber as if expecting someone else to be there, and looked blank for a moment. 'Um, this is where my assistant should be sitting. If anyone had actually bothered to give me an assistant.'

'I tend to pick mine up on the job,' said the Doctor, dabbing gingerly at his nose. 'They come in very handy, I find.'

'It's a good one, I hope it recovers.'

'You what?'

'Your nose.' She smiled. 'Good for sniffing out trouble, I'll bet.'

'Um – yes. You could say that.' He smiled back at this most unstuffy of officers. Her hair was dyed blonde and hung to her shoulders. Her own nose was long and straight, and she had a gently pointed chin. But her eyes really took his attention, blue-green and vivacious. 'How d'you do?' he said. 'Sir John Smith, Scientific Adviser. To the Admiralty, actually.'

'Are you indeed?' Vida's hands strayed to straighten her smart jacket. 'I'm sorry I wasn't here to welcome you, you and your…?'

'Oh, I'm here on my own.'

'You are?'

'I am.' He showed her the psychic paper. 'So, listen, could you direct me to where the trouble actually is?'

Vida frowned. 'I'm sorry?'

'You know. Those bits of the *Ascendant* brought back from the deeps.' He gently massaged his nose. 'I mean, I can't sniff them out for myself, now, can I?'

'I suppose not.' She parked herself on the empty desk and looked at him thoughtfully. 'So why did you want to see *me*, Sir John?'

'I didn't,' he said. 'Er, not when I know you must be so busy. I mean, liaising with people all day long… and without an assistant…'

'It is difficult,' she sighed, gripping the edge of the desk with both hands, and leaned back casually. 'I mean, we've got all these army types getting in the way, *so* paranoid about intruders... Rear Admiral Crayshaw creaking about the place, hushing everything up so no one will talk to me – and a Vice Admiral coming over from Norfolk tomorrow who's inspecting the wreck ...'

'Norfolk!' The Doctor beamed. 'I love it in Norfolk. So flat! Walk all day and never get out of breath. Ever done the Elvis Experience at Yarmouth?'

Vida cleared her throat. 'That would be Norfolk, Virginia. Largest naval base in the world. Main port on the Eastern Seaboard.'

'Ah.' The Doctor clicked his tongue. 'I should probably have known that, shouldn't I?'

'Probably,' she agreed. 'But to be honest, I first had my suspicions about you when my PC read your pass card as belonging to Sergeant Jodie North on perimeter security detail – whatever your forged ID might say.'

'Ah again. Part two of the previous "ah".'

'You see, since I *don't* have an assistant, it's helpful for me to know who's entered my little waiting room,' she explained.

'Yeah, I can see that would come in handy.' The Doctor blew out his cheeks, shoved his hands in his pockets. 'On top of that, I probably look a bit young to have been knighted, don't I?'

Vida nodded. 'There was that too.'

An uncomfortable silence ensued.

'I'm the Doctor, by the way.'

'Hello.'

'You'll be calling security, then?'

'Already have.' She slid off the desk. 'Panic button under here –'

'– which you set off while leaning back in that cool and understated manner! Very good. Oh, *very* good.' The Doctor nodded approvingly – and lunged for the outer door. 'See ya!'

'Wait!' Vida called after him. 'Who are you working for? Why did you really come here?'

But the Doctor was already running down the corridor. Security would be swarming everywhere in another few moments. Should he take the stairs, the lift or a window?

The windows were no good. No convenient fire escapes or helpful drainpipes out there, just a two-storey jump on to a gravel-strewn roof.

The lift was humming. Someone was coming up. Several someones in khaki, most likely.

He threw open the fire door to the stairs, which were echoing already with the clump of boots on concrete.

The Doctor was trapped.

FIVE

Seconds later, the corridor was bulging with armed soldiers. Vida Swann peeped out from her doorway and shook her head at the overkill.

'No sign of the intruder,' one of the troops reported.

'Strengthen the guard on the main entrance, and make sure all the fire exits are covered,' said the squad leader. 'Hit the main alarms. We'll fan out and check the other levels.' His troops parted as he turned and strode up to Vida. 'The intruder was unarmed?'

'Yes, I'm sure he was,' said Vida. 'He was just a harmless crank.'

'When we've bagged him,' said the squad leader as a siren howled into deafening life, '*we'll* be the judge of that.'

'We?' she shouted, covering her ears. 'Don't let Crayshaw hear you might be thinking for yourselves.'

The squad leader smiled. 'He's on his way up to talk to you.'

'Oh, good.' Vida smiled back. Then she slammed her office door in his face.

* * *

Unable to take the stairs, the lift or the windows, the Doctor had taken the cupboard.

It was a stationery cupboard, perched at the end of the corridor near the lift doors. Squashed up against fax paper, Post-its and stacks of biros in an assortment of colours, the Doctor held his breath as the lift doors opened and soldiers poured out into the narrow space.

It wouldn't take them long to realise he must be hiding somewhere on this level. Which was why he slipped out of the cupboard behind them and into the lift before the double doors had time to slide closed again. No Derek this time, so the Doctor stabbed the ground-floor button himself. Hardly taxing – why did they need a security guard in the lift, anyway?

Then he saw the sheer metal plate beneath the working controls, like a covering. It was locked and wouldn't budge, so he fished out his sonic screwdriver. The tool's bulbous tip glowed blue as ultrasonic frequencies bombarded the workings of the lock.

The lift had barely reached the second floor before the plate fell open – to reveal five more buttons, none of them marked. Intrigued, the Doctor changed the settings on the screwdriver and cancelled out his ground-floor choice. It suddenly seemed that he could go down further. Far further.

'What lies beneath?' he wondered aloud as the lift continued its descent.

Rose had her mobile up against one ear and Anne's head lolling against the other, as she and Mickey walked her unsteadily down a quiet back street. The old woman seemed to be drifting in and out of awareness, as if she was happiest in some other place that only she could see.

The thrum of the connected tone purred in Rose's ear, then a click. 'Hello, Mum? It's me.'

'Where've you been?' The classic Jackie Tyler greeting. In the old days it was hurled at her after stumbling through the door in the early hours after a night out with Keish and Shareen. That she still got it now after fighting googly-eyed monsters or facing off mean military types was comforting in a weird sort of way. 'Rose, you all right?'

'I'm fine. Almost home.'

'What happened to you? Thought you were coming round this afternoon?'

'Well, Keish was in a bit of a state and then I –'

'It's that Doctor again, isn't it?' Rose rolled her eyes at her mum's disapproving tone. 'He's dragged you off on one of his "adventures".'

'Mum, something weird's going on.'

'When *isn't* it, I'd like to know?'

Anne groaned suddenly, turned her head from Rose.

'Who's that?' Jackie demanded. 'Who have you got there?'

'Can we come round, me and Mickey? There's this old woman, right, she's had a funny turn. Needs a bed for the night.'

'Running a doss house now, am I? Well, sorry, sweetheart, but I can't. I've got Dennis coming round tonight –'

'Dennis? I thought he was well out of the picture!'

'Well, he said he never meant it. And a dotty old lady

floating round the place won't exactly get him in the mood to make it up to me, will it?'

'All right, whatever. I'll catch you later, yeah?'

'Just take care of yourself, Rose. Don't get into trouble.'

Bit late for that, she thought. 'Same goes for you. He's got more arms than an octopus, that Dennis.'

'Tell me about it!' said Jackie dreamily. 'Bye!'

Rose sighed and slipped the mobile back in her pocket. 'So much for giving Anne my old bed.'

'It'll have to be my place after all,' said Mickey. He'd drunk most of a big bottle of water and was looking slightly better for it. 'The way she is now, she won't even notice the sheets ain't been changed for a couple of…' He caught the accusing look on Rose's face. 'Um, weeks.'

'Let me go,' Anne whispered hoarsely. 'Let me go to him.'

Rose tightened her grip on the old woman's hand. 'Have a bit of a rest first, yeah?'

'I want to go back!' the old woman said, more loudly. A couple across the street looked over, curious.

Rose bit her lip. What were they supposed to do, hold her against her will? 'Have a cup of tea first. Get your strength.'

'I know you mean well,' said Anne, suddenly lucid. 'But you don't understand. No one could ever understand.'

'Yeah. Yeah, they could.' Rose stopped walking. 'Mickey, we've got to take her to Keisha's.'

'What?'

'You heard her. Someone who understands! They've both lost someone on that ship – it could be good for them to meet each other.'

'Fine,' said Mickey. 'I'll go with you to the door, but no way am I having anything to do with her.'

Rose sighed. 'I'll bet she's really sorry about what she did, Mickey.'

'Yeah, well, so am I.' He looked away, quickened his step a little, and that was the end of the conversation.

Vida stood in her office, trying to compose herself. Crayshaw always unnerved her, and she couldn't really work out why. He was old, cold and uncompromising, but there were enough of his type around and she was well used to them. Dealing with difficult people didn't faze her, she enjoyed the challenge. So what was it about *him*?

The inevitable beep sounded from her computer: CRAYSHAW, JOHN ANTHONY, REAR ADMIRAL, CLEARANCE A1. He was here. Vida sat down on her chair and straightened the knot of her tie.

Crayshaw entered without knocking – a habit of his, like wearing dark glasses indoors and that stupid scarf around his neck. Some put it down to eccentricity, others to illness, but Vida felt it was more a deliberate attempt to put others off guard, to intimidate. He might play the old, frail naval hero when it suited, but there was a stubborn strength about him the years could not remove.

She rose and nodded. 'Rear Admiral, what can I do for –'

'The intruder, Swann.' Crayshaw's voice was dry as dust. 'What can you tell me about him?'

'Very little. He said he was a doctor, but most likely he's a journalist. He wanted to know about the *Ascendant*.'

'Why did he come to you?'

'I don't know.' Vida shrugged. 'I suppose he could have seen my name in the visitors' book. I was visited by my superior this afternoon.'

'Mr Dolan, yes.' Crayshaw made no attempt to disguise his displeasure. 'I ran into him on his way out of the building, had a talk.' He nodded to himself. 'Mr Dolan pulled many high-ranking strings to get you an office here.'

'Is there a problem, sir?'

'I am attempting to maintain secrecy around a major incident at sea, Swann. I view your presence here, and the comings and goings of your colleagues, as a possible potential security breach.'

Vida raised her eyebrows. 'With respect, sir, as an officially recognised affiliate group with a vested interest, we have full security clearance and every right to be here. Our research and development team were conducting extremely important tests on the *Ascendant* when she went down. Naturally we are interested in retrieving data relating to those tests, and the chemicals involved.' She decided to match him for honesty and plain speaking. 'Frankly, I don't understand your reluctance to let our own scientists confer with those based here. Surely by pooling our resources –'

'We have the situation well in hand,' said Crayshaw flatly. 'And for what it's worth, you're wasting your time trawling that stretch of the German Ocean where the *Ascendant* sank –'

'German Ocean?' She stared at him blankly.

He looked almost uncomfortable for once. 'As once that body of water was known.'

For a moment, Vida considered telling him what they had found out. But no. He wouldn't share his own secrets, so why should she give him hers? 'With respect, sir, I don't believe you have personal jurisdiction over the North Sea. But may I ask why you have forbidden the wreck recovery team leaders to talk to me?'

'They are forbidden to talk to *anyone* for the duration of this inquiry.'

'And why am I barred even from boarding the tug moored outside this building? I mean, what possible value can there be in maintaining a veil of secrecy over that heap of –'

'There is value in it, Swann. Believe me.' He took an intimidating step closer. 'When our business is concluded the findings will be made public – and I assure you we shall hold nothing back.' His face twitched in an attempt at a smile. 'Until then, I feel it best you conduct your affairs elsewhere.'

'But you can't –'

'An unauthorised imposter made directly for your office.'

'Yes, and I raised the alarm!'

'I have already told your Mr Dolan that to avoid further embarrassment to all parties, you should work elsewhere, away from these premises.'

'And what did he say?'

'I fancy he saw things my way.'

'Did he, now.' Vida felt like clonking the old fool over the head with her desk lamp. *What are you trying to hide?* she wanted to yell in his wrinkly face.

'I trust you will discuss the matter with him as soon as you are able,' he said, turning and crossing to the door.

She saluted him – a two-fingered salute to his disappearing back, as the door swung shut behind him. 'Oh, yes,' she breathed, picking up the phone. 'I'll discuss it all right.'

The Doctor had gone down as far as he could. The lift doors wouldn't open at first – there was probably some sort of code required – but a little friendly persuasion with the sonic screwdriver did the trick.

He emerged into a massive high-tech hangar. It was the size of a football pitch. The floor and walls were tiled in antiseptic white, gleaming in the floodlights that peppered the ceiling. The huge floorspace was divided up into sterile work zones by swathes of clear plastic or towering glass cubicles. In each was a hulking segment of ship, pored over by bustling figures in white hazard suits.

'An underground lair!' the Doctor muttered happily. 'Ooh, the sneaky devils.'

So this was why the *Ascendant* was towed all the way here. While they downplayed the incident up on the surface, down here the ship was subjected to the closest possible scrutiny in a secret military citadel. But why?

At least there were no alarms going off down here. They wouldn't figure on him being able to make it this far. Not yet, anyway. He strode up to one of the great glass cubicles and studied the chunk of ship contained inside.

'That's weird,' he muttered.

'Who are you?' A short, middle-aged man in a hazard suit had spotted him and was scurrying over. 'What are you doing here?'

'Sir John Smith –' the Doctor began. 'Er, Sir John Smith's *son*. Dr John Smith Junior, Scientific Adviser, that's me. Come to help.'

'Well, my name's Huntley and I've never heard of you.' He pulled off his protective helmet to reveal a balding head and a fierce myopic stare. 'You have a red pass, of course.'

'Think I'd go anywhere without it? So, what's going on here, then? I can see the advantages of dismantling the *Ascendant* for close study of the separate sections. For one thing, you'd never fit a battleship in that lift.' The Doctor leaned in towards the scientist, assumed a confidential air. 'But this ship hasn't been dismantled, has it? It's been *carved up*. Chopped into neat slices like a huge, ship-shaped sausage. So how have you done that, then, eh?' He gestured to the section before them. 'I'd love to know. In this bit alone you've bisected metal inches thick, electrical components, even bolts and rivets, and yet the edges are completely smooth – no trace of trauma in the surrounding matter. That sort of technology shouldn't exist for another hundred years – so where did *you* find it?'

Huntley stared at him. 'Well, if you don't know the answer to that, Dr Smith, you're precious little use to us as an adviser.'

'Oh? How come?'

'This is how we found the *Ascendant*, lying on the sea bed,' he said. 'We didn't cut the ship up into pieces. Something else did.'

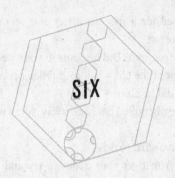

SIX

'Hi,' said Rose, forcing a big smile as Keisha opened the door. 'Said I'd come back later. Are you OK?'

Keisha just stared, her red puffy eyes narrowing to slits. 'What've you brought *him* here for?'

Mickey glared back. 'Yeah, right, never mind the strange old lady, Rose, what am *I* doing here?'

'Please let us in, Keish,' said Rose, her arm still tight round Anne. 'We need your help.'

Keisha stepped back, let the door open wider. Rose and Mickey helped Anne inside, through the cluttered hallway into the gloomy living room. Though the curtains had been drawn, Rose noticed at once that the TV had been shifted from the corner along with a stack of dog-eared magazines and CDs. Taking pride of place now in the centre of the cleared space was a congealing plate of beefburgers and beans. So much for Keisha's tea.

'What's going on?' Keisha watched them as they manhandled Anne on to the saggy couch. 'Who's she? Where'd you find her?'

Rose paused for a moment. 'Her son was on board the *Ascendant*, like Jay.'

'Have you seen him? Did he come to you?' Keisha fell to her knees in front of the old woman, grabbed her roughly by the hand. 'I *said*, did he come –'

Mickey angrily pulled her hand away. 'She's not well. Leave her alone.'

'Don't tell *me* what to do –'

'Or what? You'll get your mates to try and rough me up again?' Mickey straightened up, looked at Rose. 'I told you this was bad news. I'm out of here.'

'You *are* not,' Rose snapped. 'Now listen to me, both of you… I know you've never got on. And Keish, Mickey told me –'

'What? *What* did he tell you?'

'About what you did to him.'

'You and that lynch mob!' Mickey jumped in. 'Every time I walked out of that police station you had people waiting to put me in hospital!'

'Yeah, all that.' Rose held up her hands for peace. 'That was wrong, Keish. I know you were just upset about me going and all that, but –'

'Rose, you –'

'*But*,' she repeated, 'that's all done, it's over. And right now there's something freaky going on and I've got to get my head round it.'

'Get you!' said Mickey quietly.

'I have, though. And I'm gonna need you both on my side. So no more fighting tonight, OK?'

Mickey and Keisha looked at each other.

Then Mickey looked away. 'I really need some water. I'm parched.'

She shrugged. 'Kitchen's through there. You'll have to wash up a glass.'

He nodded and stalked off.

'Thanks,' Rose mouthed at Keisha, and crouched down in front of Anne. 'You all right?'

'Did she see her son, Rose?' Keisha seemed more controlled now. 'Did he come to her?'

'Peter asked me for help,' said Anne, staring at the plate in the corner of the room. 'He was so sad. He needed my help. Needed me to come to him…'

Keisha nodded urgently. 'Before the feast, yeah?'

Anne looked at Keisha, slow compassion spreading over her lined face. 'Yes, that's right. I thought your friend was only humouring me, but…'

'Jay was my brother,' said Keisha.

'We both saw him,' Rose said nervously.

'He'll come to you again, dear, when he's found his strength.' The tweedy old woman seemed so out of place amid the ramshackle tat of Keisha's living room, yet so self-assured. 'You won't be able to tempt him here.'

Rose glanced back at the cleared space and the cold plate of food. With a shiver she realised it was sat on the spot where the ghost had first appeared. 'That lot's for Jay?'

'They were always his favourites,' said Keisha, welling up. 'I used to cook them for him when Mum went. If he's worried about this feast thing, I thought maybe some food…'

Rose put her arms round her friend and held her tight. Mickey came out of the kitchen with a glass of water, crossed awkwardly to a chair and sat in it.

As he did so, Rose realised that every chair had been turned towards that same spot where the telly had been. She could feel Keisha carefully shifting round in the embrace, desperate to face that way too, just in case.

Anne smiled serenely, as if there was some creepy kinship between her and Keisha now. 'When our loved ones come again,' she said softly, 'we will be ready.'

The Doctor was acutely aware that Huntley was waiting to be impressed, and that the man's patience was growing thinner than his hair. 'So, the whole ship was found lying in pieces, right?'

'Of course.' Huntley frowned. 'Haven't you been briefed? Who were you told to contact when you got here?'

'Crayshaw mentioned your name to me.'

'He did?' Huntley seemed pleased but baffled.

'Bit odd, isn't it – a rear admiral taking personal charge of a situation like this, leading the troops? Don't you reckon?'

'Crayshaw was appointed to handle it.' He shrugged, as if that settled the matter. 'You're sure he didn't direct you to talk to Hempshaw? He's in charge of –'

'Hempshaw? The very thought!' The Doctor put a conspiratorial arm around Huntley. 'Hempshaw in charge? Yeah, right. We all know that results are needed – and that the men "in charge" aren't delivering. That's why I'm here.' He nodded, encouragingly. 'Bit of a shake-up, see?'

'Er...'

'We need to look at the problem afresh. New ideas, that's what we need. Fresh thinking. So! What sort of technology could do this? Hydrogen fused anti-cellularisation is my bet.'

'Hydrogen *what*?'

'You know. Goes to work on matter at an atomic level.'

'Some sort of weapon?'

'More of a state of mind. It can be used to damage and destroy, but primarily it *reworks* matter. Re-engineers it.' The Doctor gestured to one of the hunks of ship. 'Look at those clean edges! You could slice a banana on those. That's not some heavy-handed attack. That's craftsmanship, real craftsmanship.'

Huntley looked bemused. 'Craftsmanship?'

'Well, crafts*alienship*, might be a better word. Or *crafty-aliens' ship* even!'

'You're mad!'

'What's mad is to think that any humans in this time could develop hydrogen fused anti-cellularisation, let alone employ it successfully hundreds of feet under the sea,' the Doctor assured him. 'When the ship was discovered in its various sections, was there any life on board?'

'You *must* know that all the crew were lost!'

The Doctor shook his head gravely. 'I'm not talking about the crew.'

Then a klaxon burst into a deafening wail, echoing and re-echoing about the enormous, vaulted hangar. Red lights in the roof flashed on and off, spilling crimson shadows over the white space. The scientists started scurrying about like ants with a large stick poking out of their nest.

'Watch out – intruders about.' The Doctor raised his voice over the din. 'So, anyway, these huge great chunks of ship – bit big to fit in the passenger lift or slide down the stairs. You must have some way of transporting cargo down from the river.'

Huntley nodded distractedly, staring round the hangar as his colleagues left their various projects and began to congregate in the central space. 'It's a largely automated handling system. The underside of the tug locks on to a conveyance chamber concealed beneath the surface of the river. Hydraulic platforms take the cargo down an intake shaft into the main unloading bay, and from there...' He cleared his throat, lowered his voice, uncomfortable. 'Erm... everyone's staring at us.'

'My fly's not undone, is it? No. So why... oh, hang on. You don't think that they think that I'm the intruder, do you?' The Doctor grimaced. 'Tch! Typical of the kind of antiquated thinking we're dealing with here! No wonder Crayshaw sent me to see you, Huntley...'

Suddenly the lift doors slid open – to reveal half a dozen armed soldiers.

'Fresh ideas, that's what's needed.' The Doctor shook Huntley warmly by the hand. 'And I'm fresh out of them, so I'll do what I normally do in situations like this. Run!' He turned and legged it. 'Unloading bay this way, is it?'

The soldiers, with a depressing lack of originality but a great deal of nippiness, made straight for him. The Doctor ran towards a set of oversized metal doors at the far side of the chamber, labelled DECONTAMINATION. Made sense – the sort of stuff that was sent here for study, you needed to make sure it was clean before you got stuck in. He started sonicking the second he was in range – it triggered another alarm, but this one was small fry next to the pandemonium of the main klaxons. The doors slid slowly open to reveal a featureless white chamber with a set of identical doors directly opposite.

'In for a penny, in for a pound,' decided the Doctor. Another quick squizz with the screwdriver, yet another alarm in the mix, and the next doors opened in just the same way – only these ones gave on to a wide access corridor, damp and dirty and dingily lit, strafed with heavy-duty scuffs and gouge-marks.

The Doctor ran through. The soldiers were nearly on top of him, raising their weapons to fire. A quick flick to a higher sonic setting and the screwdriver sent the heavy quarantine doors flying together as if suddenly magnetised. With a sonorous clunk, they slammed shut.

'Ace-a-mundo,' he cried, and then frowned. 'A word I shall hopefully never use again.'

Deftly scrambling the motor circuits to lock the doors in place, the Doctor puffed out a sigh of relief. But as he breathed in again, his nose twitched. There was a salty reek in the air, together with something else he couldn't place. As he moved further along the gloomy corridor, his sneakers splashed in shallow, mucky puddles. He stooped, dipped a finger in one and gingerly licked it clean. 'Saltwater,' he murmured. 'Like the sea. But if this is the route down from the river… how come?'

A loud pounding noise had started up behind him as the soldiers tested the strength of the metal doors. There was no turning back, that was for sure. The question was, could he get out the same way that the cargo got in?

'One way to find out.' With a grin, the Doctor rushed on into the darkness.

Huntley edged uneasily into the scrum of his fellow scientists as Rear Admiral Crayshaw stalked from the lift and into the workshop. The alarms had shut off now, thank God, but his head was still pounding with the useless boom of the soldiers as they attacked the heavy decontamination chamber doors. Somehow, Crayshaw's footsteps on the tiled flooring rang out still louder as he approached.

'What's the delay with getting those doors open?' he demanded.

'Intruder jammed them somehow,' called one of the marines.

Crayshaw rounded on the scientists. 'Who spoke with the intruder?'

Huntley could feel the sweat oozing down his back. Working in these secret military establishments, you got used to the thunder and fury of the big bosses with their permanent migraines. He knew there was no way out of the firing line, and took a step forward. 'I did, sir.'

For a moment Crayshaw ignored him. 'I need those doors open at once,' he barked at the scientists. 'Everyone who's qualified, jump to it.'

A handful of systems analysts scuttled away. Huntley watched them leave with envy.

'Now, then, Huntley,' said Crayshaw, tightening the scarf about his neck as if he felt the cold. 'Why did you approach the intruder?'

'He looked... well, conspicuous, sir.'

'Why did you not raise the alarm at once?'

'He had a red pass card, sir.' *Well, he said he did.* 'And he said you had sent him here yourself. He mentioned you by name, and I thought –'

Crayshaw waved away his excuses. 'What did you tell him?'

'Nothing, sir. He told me things, in fact.' Huntley shrugged. 'Misinformation, I'm sure. A lot of wild nonsense. I mean, why would he –'

An impatient sigh. 'What did he tell you?'

'He put the dissection of the ship down to anti-cellularisation.'

Most of the military types were lost at the first whiff of jargon, particularly the older types. But Crayshaw seemed unfazed. 'Go on.'

'Well, his mad theory was that matter was being reworked at an atomic level, fused by hydrogen.' Huntley paused, thoughtful. 'Though if hydrogen *could* be harnessed as the power source, the sea would be a perfect medium in which to operate such a –'

'Do you now believe there could be any truth in this "wild nonsense"?' Crayshaw inquired.

Huntley could almost feel his colleagues shrinking back from him, disowning him utterly. 'Fresh ideas,' he said quietly, smoothing over his few remaining hairs. 'That's what's needed here. In the absence of conventional explanations –'

'– we should accept the ramblings of an unidentified intruder?'

Huntley could feel his legs slowly turning to jelly. He spoke quickly before they could give way completely. 'I simply believe in keeping a mind open to all possibilities, sir.'

Unexpectedly, Crayshaw smiled. 'Excellent, Huntley.' He rounded on the other scientists. 'You should all take a leaf from this man's book! Not one of you has come up with a satisfactory explanation as to what can have happened to this vessel. I need answers, gentlemen! I need commitment!' He jabbed a finger at the decon chamber, where the systems boys were clustering like aphids around a bud. 'And I need those doors open at once!'

The more electrically-minded scientists headed over to see what they could do. Huntley was about to try and lend a hand himself when Crayshaw stopped him. The black lenses of the old man's glasses, brightly peppered with the reflected lights, made it hard to look at him.

'When does your shift end tonight, Huntley?'

'Eleven, sir.'

'I think perhaps we need to talk. Wait for me here. Don't leave before I come to you. Understood?'

'Yes, sir,' said Huntley, trying to hide how startled he was.

Crayshaw gave him a slightly sickly smile. Then, with a protesting screech, the decon doors opened to ragged applause. The old boy stalked off without another word. 'I'll lead the way,' he shouted. 'Fall in.'

Huntley watched him go, chewing his lip. There was a whiff of advancement about this invitation, he was sure of it.

Despite everything, the mysterious Dr Smith had been right all along.

And if he'd been right about that…

Huntley shuffled off, ignoring the dark looks and mutterings in his direction from the remaining scientists. His mind was tussling with unruly new ideas, and inside he was shining as bright as the lights.

The Doctor splashed on through the dingy access corridor. The fluorescent lights in the ceiling were caked with grime, and many had conked out. His shoes were soaked, and his sodden trouser legs clung to his ankles.

After a sharp turn, the corridor opened up into a large, dark, circular chamber. 'Hello,' the Doctor murmured. 'A significant bit. Or do I mean pit?'

There was no ceiling. He was stood at the bottom of an enormous vertical borehole through the concrete. He decided it must be the cargo lift shaft, used to ferry materials down to the secret workshops. It was impossible to know how high and far it stretched, the only lights being small white maintenance bulbs, flanking an inspection ladder at intervals. A huge, filthy pool was set in the centre of the floor – some kind of drainage channel for the excess river water that came down with the cargo. And yet right now it was full to the brim. It had been flooded.

From the smell of it, flooded with sea water.

'So,' the Doctor announced, his voice boomy and hollow in the near-darkness. 'Are you just a blocked drain? Or a nice little home for some special form of marine life?' He crouched down, pulled a crumpled polythene bag from his breast pocket and dipped it into the water. The water was icy cold, made his fingers tingle. 'All I need now is a goldfish,' he decided, holding up the full bag. 'Any goldfish about?'

He thought he caught a flash of movement – a ripple, dead in the centre of the dark pool. But the light was so poor, he could have imagined it. He straightened, tied a knot in the bag and placed it back in his pocket. A distant clanking sound echoed eerily from the way he had come. He knew he didn't have long.

Skirting the sinister dark pool, he hauled himself up on to the inspection ladder and started to scale the shaft. But he had barely covered a couple of rungs before he stopped still. Parts of the steel ladder were wet. From the position of the patches, they could only be hand- and footprints.

Someone sopping wet had been here before him only recently, climbing into the dank darkness.

Lying in wait.

'Maybe *they've* got the goldfish,' the Doctor reasoned.

Warily, as silently as he could, he continued up the rungs.

SEVEN

Up the Doctor went, ever higher into the cold, stifling gloom. Freezing water dripped remorselessly down on him from high above. The metal rungs were cutting into the thin soles of his sneakers, and his arms and legs were aching with effort. The tiny white stud-lights did little to dispel the inky blackness, so he kept stopping every few feet to listen out for the tell-tale sound of someone above him. Whoever they were, they hadn't dried out – his fingers kept encountering the wet residue.

He held his breath and listened: nothing save the sprightly thump of his two hearts pulsing in his ears.

Finally he came up against a solid metal barrier, blocking his progress upwards. Since it meshed into metal grooves on either side of the shaft, this had to be the cargo platform, waiting to fetch down whatever was loaded on to it. And since there were no controls at the bottom of the shaft, it must be controlled from the tug up above. But how was he going to get past it? He groped with one hand along the underside of the platform. There should surely be an –

'Inspection hatch,' the Doctor hissed, his hands closing around a metal handle. It felt warm and sticky under his fingers as he twisted, released the catch. A circular hatch cover pivoted clear. A pale light shone from within, illuminating the shaft.

The Doctor saw his hand was now sticky with blood.

'Curiouser and curiouser,' he said. 'Not to mention nastier and grosser.'

He would have to lean across and pull himself up through the hole in the platform's underside. That would leave him dangling over a drop of at least 300 feet, while whoever had got here ahead of him could well be waiting just out of view – bleeding and very, very wet.

He started at a sudden volley of noises far below: the muffled rap of an order, well-drilled footsteps, the crack of hefty safety catches coming off. Then an uneasy silence.

The Doctor decided to chance leaning over towards the open hatchway – just as the gunfire started.

'Well, this is fun,' Mickey announced, and Rose gave him a look. She couldn't blame him, though. They'd been sitting together in tense silence for a good hour, waiting for something scary to happen. Although from the sound of soft snoring, Anne had opted out of the nerves marathon for now.

Through the window, Rose was dimly aware of the world going on around them. Boys shouted to each other in the street, kicked cans around. Dance music pumped posily from someone's car stereo. A gang of girls clopped down the pavement in their heels, excited, laughing. It was a Friday night. Once upon a time, that alone would have been a cause for celebration. It would have been unthinkable to stay in on a Friday.

Keisha used to start texting her and Shareen on a Tuesday and they would plan their big night in crazy detail – hair, what to wear, which bar to kick off in. Which clubs, of course – that was a serious business. You had to rate the DJs on how good they were compared to how cute they looked, and the arguments and the laughter went on well into the night.

Together, Rose and her mates had always made Friday come early and last most of the week. That was the sort of time-travel the Doctor would never understand in a billion years. And yet it all seemed so distant to her now. She was only nineteen, but being with the Doctor had made her grow up so much.

Or maybe grow *old* so fast.

'I'm gonna pop out, get some fresh air,' Mickey announced. 'I want to check the paper, see if there's anything more being said about the ghost ship, people disappearing and that.'

'That's a good idea,' Rose said.

'Does that newsagent's on the corner still open late?'

Keisha nodded. 'Maybe not today, though. Something happened there today, didn't it?'

Rose nodded. 'The Doctor said some of the customers collapsed or something. There were ambulances and…' She trailed off. 'Oh, God. How thick am I?'

Mickey frowned. 'What?'

'Just before… before Jay appeared, those people in the newsagent's round the corner collapsed or something. And

65

when Anne saw her son, those soldiers went down.'

'And I felt really sick.' Mickey nodded. 'So what does that mean, they're linked?'

'Jay wouldn't hurt no one,' said Keisha flatly.

Rose looked at her sympathetically. 'He might not mean to, but –'

'He wouldn't!' Her face darkened. 'What makes you think you know so much about everything, Rose? Just 'cause you've been *travelling* –'

'Oh, and what, the Doctor's given me airs and graces? You sound like my mum!'

'Oi!' hissed Mickey, pointing at Anne. 'You're gonna wake her up.'

Rose and Keisha both fell silent. The distant carefree blare of music and people having fun drifted in through the dirty windows.

'Why can't things just be like they used to be?' whispered Keisha.

Rose didn't have an answer.

Slowly she got up. 'I think I'll try and find out what happened in that newsagent's.'

Mickey frowned. 'I'll come with you.'

'Not worth it, I'll only be five minutes.' She pointed to Anne, mouthing, *Look after her.* 'I'll bring you that paper, yeah?'

'But I'm the one who wanted some fresh air.' He looked hurt. 'You think I can't handle this.'

'You got sick last time, remember? If anything weird happens again, you could get it worse.'

'Well, what about you? What if *you* get sick this time?'

'Just five minutes.' She turned and crossed to the front door. 'Take care.'

'Just 'cause you're his mate, it don't make you indestructible,' Mickey called after her. But she had closed the door, and her footsteps were already fading away.

Mickey glanced down at Keisha, still kneeling on the floor in front of the chair. She was watching him.

'Here we are again, then,' she said coolly. 'Alone at last.'

As the harsh death-rattle from a dozen light support weapons started up, the Doctor lunged for the rim of the open hatchway. The sound of the gunfire, distorted and magnified by the cavernous stone acoustics, thundered all around him as he just managed to grab hold. He dangled in the darkness, clinging on by his fingertips as bullets burst past. Concrete shrapnel and shards of metal exploded into the air, stinging his skin.

Abruptly the firing stopped. His ears still ringing in the aftermath, the Doctor pulled himself up through the inspection hatch and lay face down, the metal floor cold and wet against his skin. The cargo lift doors were open, and he saw the platform was aligned with the floor of another enormous access tunnel, waiting for the next load to be wheeled on board.

But there was no one here waiting for him. In the dim lighting of the access tunnel the Doctor could see spatters of bloody water on the platform's scarred and grimy surface.

A further sharp chatter of gunfire broke out, and the Doctor felt the bullets' impact as they pounded into the underside of the platform. Then a man's voice rose in anger, and even the echoes seemed somehow clipped and dry with age.

'Get up above and alert the perimeter patrols,' he said. 'I want that tug well covered, but no one is to board it until I say so.'

'At once, sir.'

The Doctor nodded to himself. *Rear Admiral Crayshaw, I presume.*

'The rest of you, fan out and search back the way we came.' A pause, and then, before the eerie echoes could die down, 'I will check the pool myself.'

The Doctor screwed up his nose. 'Good luck.' He clambered to his feet and was about to get going when he heard another voice echo spookily up to him. It was softer, more sibilant, a female voice maybe, rising like a sudden mist over the black waters.

'Remain selective who you take from. For now, we need these soldiers alive.'

Do you now, thought the Doctor. *Personally, I could do with them somewhere else. Just who are you anyway?*

'We will capture the escaping one. Bind him. Bring him back. He must play his part to swell the numbers at the feast.'

'Me?' the Doctor murmured. 'Or whoever got up here first?' Burning with curiosity, for a lunatic split-second the Doctor contemplated popping back down the shaft to see what was happening. But he knew he couldn't afford to stay eavesdropping. Whoever had left the blood and water was still at large, hurt and most likely scared as all hell. A fellow fugitive, it seemed – but what had he escaped *from*? The Doctor knew he must find him fast and get up to the tug's deck before the soldiers completely cut off their only chance of escape.

So he stole away along the winding access tunnel, splashing once more through freezing, dirty water. It got deeper the further along he went – salt-stinking, and already up to his shins. But it had to be passable, he thought, rounding a corner. There was still no sign of the mysterious escapee –

Scratch that.

The Doctor came to a sloshing stop. A dark figure stood turned from him, half in shadow, hunched against a door in the wall. It shook and shivered, rasping for breath.

'Hello!' the Doctor called. 'You OK? Hurt yourself?'

The figure didn't react.

'It's all right, we're in the same boat. Literally, as it happens! But I'm not talking about the tug, I mean we're both in hot water. Um, metaphorically, this time. It's actually freezing cold, isn't it? Or is that just me?'

The figure ignored him. The swirling water was almost up to their waists by now.

'So, anyway, I can probably open that door. Who are you? I'm the Doctor.'

The figure froze. 'Doctor?'

'Yeah. Well, no, not *literally* a doctor, but I –'

'Can… can you help me?' It was a man's voice, hoarse, south Londonish. 'Can you?'

The Doctor waded through the water towards him. 'S'all right. Show me where you hurt.'

The man spun round to face him. The Doctor stopped in his tracks.

It was a young black man, tall and burly. The sleeve of his ragged blazer was braided with the single stripe of a naval rating. His face was in shadow, but thick bloody welts sat like gorging slugs on his cheeks and neck. Clots had oozed down to stain his white square collar crimson.

'Where have you come from, then?' the Doctor murmured. 'What have they done to you?'

'I had to get out of there,' the young man said, starting to shake again. 'I can't stop them coming. You're a doctor, *you* make them stop. Make them stop coming.'

'We'll figure something out,' the Doctor assured him. 'But right now we have to get out of here.' He held out a hand. 'So come on, move away from the door, let me see…'

'It's my little sister, right? And my mum.' The young rating edged forwards, still shaking, and the Doctor saw his face for the first time. There were three deep score marks in the skin of each cheek, twitching and puckering like baby mouths, spitting and sucking down air.

And his eyes were huge, blank and bulging from his sockets, a dull smooth silver-white like enormous pearls.

The Doctor stared at the man sadly, kept his hand outstretched. 'Come on,' he said quietly. 'It's OK.'

'Mum, my little Keisha…' The rating was wheezing for breath, and a bloody tear squeezed out from one of his pearly eyes. 'I don't want to hurt them, but I can't… can't stop it…'

'Oh, blimey,' said the Doctor as the penny dropped with a nasty clatter. 'You're Keisha's brother. Jay, isn't it?'

'Keish…?'

'I'm a friend of Rose. You know her, don't you? Rose Tyler? Yeah, course you do.' As Jay stumbled forwards, choking, an anger as cold as the churning water stirred inside the Doctor. 'Who did this to you?'

Hang on – *churning*?

'They're coming,' Jay hissed, hugging himself. 'I'll never stop them coming. Can't get away.'

'We *can* get away,' the Doctor insisted. The water was thickening like a strong, salty soup as he pushed through to the door and pressed the bulb of the sonic screwdriver against the hinges. The water forced it open, surged through to engulf the first few steps of a metal stairwell, a means for the cargo handlers to travel from tug to loading bay. 'There's not far to go now.' The Doctor climbed up the stairs, out of the sludge. 'Come on, Jay! Now!'

But Jay was convulsing, shouting wildly at the thrashing waters. The Doctor was about to go back for him when a piratical figure burst out of the waist-deep water. It was a man, pearly-eyed, dressed in material once grand and finely embroidered. His hair was black, but his face was chalk-white and bloated-looking; he looked as if he belonged to another time long since past. Then a second figure rose silently from the cold, churning liquid – a pale, thin man with a close-cropped beard. His bulging eyes gleamed like the iron cross that weighed upon his dark greatcoat, and his peaked cap bore the eagle insignia of the Third Reich *Kriegsmarine*.

Where had they sprung from? The Doctor started back down the steps.

'I'm not gonna do it!' Jay shouted, but a second later the pirate and the U-boat captain had dragged him back down beneath the freezing waters.

The Doctor splashed noisily after them, but caught a glimpse of dark movement at the corner of the access tunnel. It was as if the three figures had been swept away by some sudden, impossible current, though the water had become calm and still.

There was nothing he could do for Jay now.

'I'll be back,' the Doctor promised, then frowned. 'Or did someone already say that?' He cleared his throat. 'I shall return! No, this isn't the Philippines… I'm just going outside, I may be some time? Oh, blimey, no…'

He turned and hurried away up the steps. The soldiers must surely be waiting for him by now. At least they hadn't been ordered *on* to the tug. Why was that? Because Jay had been at large and the soldiers weren't supposed to know about him? Well, now that the poor bloke had been taken by those creatures, the coast was clear – or rather, the tug was. He emerged into a cramped ship's corridor, aware that it could be crawling with soldiers at any moment.

The Doctor ran on until he reached a locked bulkhead. With a blast of sonic blue he opened it and ducked inside, into the tug's cabin. The windows were shrouded by a heavy tarpaulin; it was anyone's guess how many soldiers out on the bank had their guns trained on him. But at least it kept out prying eyes, and perhaps he could find something of use here…

He glanced round the ship's controls. It looked to have once been a standard notch tug – connected to a specially designed cargo barge through a notch in the stern, effectively making them one ship. But some of the controls had clearly been customised; one touch-sensitive screen showed a glowing green schematic of the base of the tug, which looked to be locked on to the top of the cargo loading shaft.

And now that he came to listen, he could hear the ring of steel heels on metal. Someone was on board.

Coming his way.

The little newsagent's was a bright window in the dark of the parade. As Rose pushed inside through the door she found herself hemmed in by mags and crisps and chocolate and bog rolls. There weren't many papers left and none of them were screaming about the *Ascendant*. She hedged her bets and picked up a heavy posh one and the *Star*.

An Asian woman sat on a stool beside the till, a tired smile on her face. 'Looking for anything else, love?'

'Sort of.' Rose pushed past two grubby deep-freezes filled with pizza, falafel and ice cream. 'I heard you had ambulances here today.'

The woman grinned. 'Actually we did all right out of it. Had a real rush on the bottled water.'

'What d'you mean?'

'Advanced dehydration, the medics said. "Dangerous lack of water in the body". That's what made 'em drop. And it was weird, 'cause it weren't as if they even knew each other but they were all the same…' The woman frowned. 'Never seen that happen on *Casualty*. Anyway, must have scared all the people watching, 'cause they bought up all the water we had, still *and* sparkling.'

Rose bit her lip. She shuddered at the memory of Jay's ghost, water gushing out of his mouth, and the way the soldiers had collapsed. 'When they fell, those customers – did they sort of have fits?'

The woman nodded. 'Oh yeah, and some of them were sick and all. It was disgusting. But the medics said that's the symptoms you'd expect. But long term – not, like, in two seconds flat. They were all right before, see.'

'Yeah,' said Rose, 'I think I do.' There was a link here, had to be. But why water? Because the ship had sunk and drowned everyone aboard?

'So, you buying those papers, then?' the woman prompted.

'Oh. Yeah, sorry.' Rose reached in her pocket and handed over a couple of quid.

The woman took the coins. And then she fell backwards off the stool, collapsed in a heap together with a small avalanche of cigarette packets.

'God! Are you all right?' Rose crouched beside her, looked about for anyone who could help.

But there was only the ghost of Jay, stood shivering between the samosas and the dog-eared birthday cards. 'Help me, Rose. Come to me,' he pleaded. A stream of water poured from his nose as he gave her a tiny, hopeful smile. 'Please. Before the feast.'

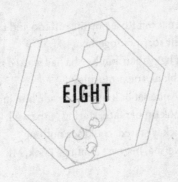

EIGHT

'You ain't told her, have you?' said Keisha. 'You ain't never told her.'

Mickey sat down carefully beside the sleeping Anne. 'No. And neither have you. Because it was nothing. Less than nothing.'

She looked at him scornfully. 'You're telling me.'

'Ancient history.'

'That's why you're so scared it's gonna come out, is it?'

'It won't. Why would you tell her? You're just as much in the wrong as me.'

'You took advantage, Mickey.'

'I never! I would never do that –'

'Thought you couldn't remember?'

Mickey buried his head in his hands. It was the truth, he couldn't. When Rose had pushed off with the Doctor for the first time, he'd just watched her disappear, he'd done nothing. And yeah, pathetic though it was, he'd gone asking round Rose's mates just in case they'd heard from her – even Keisha. She was going through a bad patch; what else was new. But she was upset about Rose pushing off too and they'd decided to drown their sorrows together.

Things got hazy then, but Keisha had wasted no time filling in the awful blanks next morning...

Suddenly Anne sat bolt upright, made him jump. She wore an ecstatic look on her face, staring at the wall. 'Peter!'

'What?' Mickey stared, could see nothing.

'Jay,' said Keisha, her eyes shining. 'Look, Mickey, he's here. It's Jay!'

'Oh, you have so got to be kidding me,' said Mickey, a shiver crawling up his back. 'There's no one there!'

But Keisha was nodding to empty space. 'Yeah. Yeah, I'll come.'

Someone was screaming upstairs, calling for help. From outside in the street too, there came frantic shouts for an ambulance. Mickey ran to the window and saw a gang of lads were lying sprawled in the road. One was being sick, another yelling into his mobile. 'Yeah, I need an ambulance! They just went down, man! I think they're dying!'

Mickey turned back, saw Anne slowly walking to the door, like a sleepwalker.

'No, you don't,' he muttered, rushing round to try to stop her. 'Anne? You gotta stop this. Whatever you can see, right, it's not real. Just a dream.'

Anne's eyes hardened as they focussed on him. 'Get off me,' she snarled, pushing him away. He stumbled over a pile of magazines, lost his balance and fell. Anne wasn't moving like a sleepwalker now. She was like a bat out of hell, heading for the front door.

'No!' Mickey shouted, jumping to his feet. But then his whole body seemed to cramp up and the sick feeling he'd had back at the bridge returned, worse than ever. He doubled up, fell to his knees. Heard the front door quietly click shut as Anne left the flat. He crawled on his hands and knees, trying to go after her, but he knew it was too late.

You messed it up.

Then he saw Keisha was making for the door as well.

'No way!' he said hoarsely. 'You ain't going too.'

'I've got to go to Jay,' she said calmly. 'I can't just leave him, can I?'

He forced himself to stand. 'Now why don't we wait for Rose to get back and we can –'

'He needs me, Mickey.' She tried to push him aside but Mickey wasn't having it a second time. He grabbed hold of Keisha and bundled her into the little bathroom, slammed the door shut. His head was throbbing, the screams and shouting were still going on upstairs and outside, and now Keisha was shrieking at him to open the door, banging it, kicking it. It took all his strength to hold it closed.

Then there was a rapping at the door. 'Keish? You all right?'

'Rose?' Mickey croaked. 'Get after Anne. She's gone.'

'She's *what*?' Rose banged at the door. 'Is Keisha all right?'

'She's gone crazy, wants out of here too. Says she saw Jay –'

'So did I, out in the shop. There's all these people collapsing…'

'I know how they feel,' said Mickey. 'Go on, get after Anne. Move!'

'Take care,' she shouted, and then she was gone.

'Take care?' The door almost jumped from his grip as Keisha yanked on it again, bellowing with rage. 'I should be *in* care.'

Gritting his teeth, he kept holding on.

Rose ran through the night-time streets. Sirens howled like wild beasts speeding closer. Electric blue flashes ate into the shadows as an ambulance tore by. She tossed her head this way and that, looking for any sign of Anne, and kept imagining she could see Jay standing there, watching her from the shadows, smiling and dripping wet.

His image hadn't hung around for long. He'd begged her to come to him, and she'd felt this urge to go after him, just like that. But it had been so long since she'd seen him last, and what she'd felt for him aged fourteen was embarrassing, just schoolgirl stuff. To hear him call to her so desperately, with that heartfelt need in his eye... it didn't quite add up to her. She couldn't quite believe he meant it.

'Please,' he'd said, one more time, and then exploded in a huge gout of water. The mags were all drenched, and Rose found herself thinking the owners would be really upset, and that jolted her memory that the Asian woman was lying on the floor and not looking good.

Rose had dialled for an ambulance – her hands were shaking so bad she could hardly hold the phone – and as soon as she had persuaded another customer to mind the woman till it came, she'd run straight back to Keisha's. If Jay had appeared to her, Keisha must have seen him too. And sure enough, Keish was freaking out, trying to get to him just like Anne was trying to get back to Peter. What the hell was going on? And where the hell was the Doctor when they needed him? If he'd got himself into trouble and needed her help…

With a tiny glimmer of cheer she realised she might just be set to kill two birds with one stone. Anne would be heading back to the bridge she'd tried to jump from before – yeah, that made sense – right on the doorstep of the Doctor's disappearance. But what if the old girl wasn't on foot? What if she'd got the bus or something?

Rose stopped running, checked her purse. Just shrapnel, a couple of quid, tops – not enough for a cab. But the cab driver wouldn't know that, and this was a matter of life and death…

She ran off in the opposite direction, towards the taxi rank.

'I have every right to be here,' Vida told herself, affecting a vague attempt at a swagger along the tug's dowdy corridors. 'I don't especially *want* to be here, but if I'm going to find out *anything* useful before I'm thrown out of this dump…'

She approached the tug's cabin, and then paused at the sound of movement. Someone was inside. More warily, she edged towards the open bulkhead…

And then the intruder peered round the doorway. Each clocked the other and jumped at the same time.

'You!' cried Vida.

'Me,' he agreed. 'And my nose for trouble. You were right, it's very good. I'm the Doctor, hello.'

'What the hell are you doing here?'

'Use your bonce, Vida! I'm trying to break out of your secret underground military citadel, what d'you *think* I'm doing here?'

'Just who are you? Press?'

'Press what? One of these?' He jabbed a button on the touch-sensitive screen.

'Very funny. You've –'

'I'll tell you what's *not* so funny,' he snapped. 'The *Ascendant*'s been taken apart like an animal for dissection by means unknown to the human race. And I've seen the result of some kind of alien vivisection experiment on one of its crew.'

She stared. 'Alien?'

'Yes, alien.' He leaned forwards and hissed the word in her face. 'Alien, alien, alien, alien, alien. You didn't know?'

'I know you're crazy,' she said.

'Then shouldn't you be scared? We're alone down here and you're fresh out of doors to throw in my face.'

'I'll find something,' she assured him, folding her arms. 'Just tell me, "Doctor". What are you trying to achieve here?'

He folded his own arms, matching her movements. 'What are your bosses trying to achieve with those sick experiments?'

She took a step closer. 'You come snooping about, try to incriminate *me* by coming to my office –'

'How many more of the crew are being held down there? What's being done to them?'

'– and now you turn up here! Don't you think you're pushing your luck?'

'Oh, I'm pushing everything!' He twirled round and hit several controls. 'Look! Look at me go! Oh, hang on –' he leaned over and flicked another switch – 'missed one.'

'Will you leave all that!' she cried. 'How the hell did you get past the soldiers? I had to show them faxed authorisation from Vice Admiral Kelper that I was allowed on board.'

'He's the one from Norfolk, Virginia, on his way to inspect the wreck?'

'He's a powerful man.'

The Doctor looked unimpressed. 'Friends in high places and monsters in low ones. You've got all bases covered, haven't you – especially the top-secret underground ones? Just what *is* happening down there?'

She hesitated. 'I don't know. Could be anything,' she admitted. 'Crayshaw won't let me anywhere near the secret stuff. He's been trying to get rid of me from the moment I showed. And thanks to you very helpfully crashing my office and making me look like I'm involved with you –'

'Steady!' His eyes twinkled. 'We only just met!'

'– he's made it very clear I'm on borrowed time here. Wants me out of the way.'

'Hence the note from the admirable Vice Admiral. Even so, I'm surprised those soldiers let you on board with this flap on.'

She shrugged. 'Seemed a bit out of it, to be honest. Especially poor old Private Jodie North, whose pass you pinched.'

He looked surprised. 'Isn't she in hospital?'

Vida shifted warily. 'Why should she be? What did you do to her?'

'Tried to help her. And her patrol. One minute they're fine, all guns and aggro – the next, they're nearly dead from advanced dehydration.'

'*What?* Come off it.'

'Weird, isn't it? I mean, that's not just me, it is weird, right? Yeah. Weird. So any recovery would be quite miraculous. Unless…' He held out a hand for silence. 'Shh!'

'What is it?' she said, frowning.

'It all comes back to the water,' he said, and now she could hear the lap of the river as it sloshed at the sides of the tug. 'Something very freaky is going on. Something in the water…'

She stiffened.

The Doctor noticed at once, of course. 'What? What did I say?'

'Nothing.'

'I did. Oh, that was a definite reaction, Vida Swann. A big fat one.'

'You're crazy,' she insisted. 'Talking about aliens –'

'You didn't run and raise the alarm this time, though, did you?' He grinned. 'Either you secretly believe me or you think I'm cute.'

'You're out of your –'

'Which is it?' He winked. 'Or is it a bit of both?'

'Those soldiers out there are fine, OK? You're just winding me up!' She crossly waved her piece of folded fax paper. 'This gave me all the leverage I needed to get inside here. Even Crayshaw can't overrule –'

'Leverage! I was almost forgetting. Lever – from *levare*, to raise!' He clicked his fingers, looked wildly around before pouncing on the biggest, chunkiest lever in the cabin. 'Well, poor old long-suffering Crayshaw must be about ready to *levare* hell round here. We'll have soldiers storming this place any moment, clomp, clomp, clomp, big boring bovver boots stepping all over our toes. Ow!'

Vida jumped as, with a sudden, snorting roar, the tug's engines started up. 'What the hell are you doing?'

'We can't get off the boat with all those soldiers outside, can we? So we'll just take her for a quick spin.'

'You can't!'

'Can too! I wasn't flicking switches just for show, you know. I've already disengaged from the cargo trailer.' He flashed her a wild grin as he crossed to the ship's wheel. 'Now then, which way should we head? I know it's a bit tricky with these tarps over the windows but –'

Suddenly gunfire rattled out. The tarp jumped and glass shattered as bullets tore through the windows. Vida threw herself to the ground, landed just beside the Doctor.

'Oh. That's a bit of a shame.' He pulled a face. 'Looks like Crayshaw doesn't want to take me alive.'

Rose kept glancing worriedly at the traffic. She'd asked the cabbie to drive round as close to the river as possible, but he was spending more time flicking between CDs for the stereo than he was looking at the road.

'Can you stop here a minute?' she asked as she noticed a small modern police station, perched on the end of St Mary's Pier as if it had grown up through the blackened brickwork. The idea of asking the police for help struck her as a weird one at first. But there was no reason why she and the Doctor had to act like lone rangers the whole time. Maybe Anne had been picked up before she could jump – in which case maybe the police could tell her where the woman was and if she was OK. 'Er, keep the meter running,' she told the cabbie. 'I won't be long.'

He was short and bulky, had to sit on a cushion to reach the pedals of his cab. 'You're not thinking of doing a runner are you, girlie?'

'Don't worry.' Rose gave him her warmest smile and pointed to the cop shop. 'If I am, I'm sure they'll soon stop me.'

The police station, though, seemed shut. She banged on the door as loud as she could, even kicked it a couple of times.

'You all right?' a voice called up to her from over the edge of the pier. She looked down below and saw a police patrol boat moored there. A middle-aged, slightly mournful-looking man was staring back up at her. 'We've had to shut the station, the river's gone mad tonight. There'll be someone at Waterloo Pier you can talk to.'

Rose was already nipping down the crumbling concrete steps. 'Can't I talk to you?'

'I'm getting the boat ready.' She could see he was stood between a tool box and an open inspection panel in the deck, grease on his face and uniform. 'She's been out of commission, awaiting repairs. But God knows we need her tonight. Sorry, miss, but I can't stop.'

'I won't get in your way,' Rose promised, tripping lightly across the jetty. 'What's your name?'

'Fraser. PC Fraser.'

'Well, PC Fraser, just thought maybe you could check something out for me on your radio or something.'

He ignored that, bent over the hatch and got on with his repairs. 'Worried about someone who's gone missing, are you? Think they've disappeared, like the papers say?'

'A woman in her fifties, called Anne. I don't know her surname, but I can describe her.' He didn't seem to be listening so she raised her voice. 'She was trying to throw herself into the river near Southwark, and I think she might try again.'

'We were down to about fifty deaths a year on the Thames,' Fraser announced. 'Faster boats, see. They let us save more people. When you think there's more than fifty-four miles of river, well, fifty deaths isn't bad.'

'S'pose you can never save everyone,' said Rose quietly.

'That's right.' He looked up, and she saw how grey and sad his eyes were. 'If they go in near bridge buttresses there are swirling currents that drag them down before you can reach them. And the bridges are high, so if your friend fell in at Southwark she'd most likely be unconscious when she hit and –'

'You're a real bundle of laughs, aren't you? Look, please, if you could just quickly check for me if she's been spotted anywhere...' For an awkward moment she thought he was about to cry. 'Hey, what's wrong?'

'They're not disappearing like the papers say. Not in that way.' He returned to the job in hand, suddenly determined. 'They've all gone into the water. Us and the soldiers, we've been doing our best trying to stop them, but we've had eyewitnesses spotting loads of people going under these last few days.'

Rose felt her stomach turn. 'Loads?'

'All sorts. Not just the flash Harrys, out to prove how tough they are. Others. Swimming, some of them, like their lives depended on it, but then…' He shook his head helplessly. 'Anyway, I told the boys at the Wapping mortuary – you'll be short-staffed, I said. You'll have a rush on.' He grunted as something gave way in the mechanism beneath the deck. 'Bodies usually pop up from the bottom within twenty-four hours of going down, you see, this time of year. You die, you sink to the bottom until the gases in your body build up and you swell –'

Rose held up a hand. 'OK, I get you.'

'In the winter it's different, might take three or four weeks. But not in spring…' He paused. 'You know how many bodies they've had brought into Wapping, miss? None.'

She stared. 'What, none at all?'

'Not a single one. So if all these people have gone under, where've all the bodies gone, eh? Who's got them?'

Rose couldn't answer him.

'They say it's something to do with that ghost ship,' said Fraser. 'Saying it's cursed. That it's… *luring* people here.'

She found she wanted to blurt out everything she knew, just to share it with someone. To tell him how the dead crew of the *Ascendant* seemed to be haunting the people they knew and loved, urging them, begging them to join them.

But no. Even if he somehow believed her, this man clearly had enough on his plate. So she gave him the censored version. 'There's something iffy going on, all right. I met this high-up old naval bloke, he was well on to this whole "throw yourself in" thing. Wanted to talk to Anne when she tried to jump. Wanted to know if anyone else like her turned up.'

'Why?' Fraser said. 'What's wrong with these people? What's *special* about them?'

She shuddered. 'I dunno.'

Fraser straightened up, wiped his hands on a rag. 'Mate of mine over at Waterloo, Fisky. He was saying there's more of them each night. That's why the marines have been brought in. Has to be *them* holding the bodies somewhere…'

'Where?'

'Fisky didn't say… couldn't say.'

'Too many secrets being kept around here,' muttered Rose. 'Can you help me? With finding Anne, I mean?'

'Sorry, love, got to get this boat on patrol. You'd best try someone at Waterloo. Though I doubt they'll have been told much themselves.' He looked at her, pale and melancholy. 'By the soldiers, I mean.'

There was a loud, ugly honking from the road up above. Her driver was getting impatient.

'I'd better push off. Taken up enough of your time, haven't I?' She forced a big grin for him. 'Good luck with it, yeah? Glad you're on the case, PC Fraser. Whatever you might think, you're a hero, dealing with this.'

He didn't answer, and she hurried back up the steps. For all the cheer in her grin, Rose was feeling worse now than she had before.

'They can't just open fire like that!' shouted Vida, scrabbling up from the floor, broken glass biting at her palms. 'Stop it!'

she yelled up through one of the broken windows. Perversely, the soldiers took that as their cue to get blasting again. 'Crew on board, you maniacs! You just saw me come in!'

''Scuse me!' The Doctor had dashed back over to the ship's controls. 'I could use a little help over here.'

Vida stared at him. 'Give it up, Doctor, they're firing at you!'

'I think you'll find they're firing at *us*.' The engines roared, the floor lurched and they were under way.

'Stop the engine!' she shouted. 'I have clearance! I have my own office – just about, anyway. Why would they be shooting at –'

'You said yourself you've been a thorn in Crayshaw's side.' He looked at her and shrugged, suddenly deadly serious. 'I think he allowed you on board so you could be killed along with me.'

She felt suddenly sick. 'Killed?'

'What do you reckon, Vida, ten to starboard?' He spun the ship's wheel with abandon as another burst of gunfire splintered teak frames and thick glass alike. The tug turned sharply, and Vida's stomach lurched with it. 'Aye, Captain!' he cried in a silly voice. 'Starboard ten, soldiers nil!'

'Why the hell would Crayshaw want to kill me?'

'Oh, it'll seem like a tragic accident – stray bullet or something. But as far as he's concerned, your being here is proof of your guilt. I mean, first we enjoy a secret tryst in your office, then I rampage through the whole secret underground base, then you meet me here – well, it's obvious, isn't it? You're trying to help me escape...'

'Circumstantial rubbish!'

'It *is* a bit dodgy.' He straightened up the tug, squinted through a hole in the tarp made by one of the bullets. 'Dodgy as trying to steer this thing blind.'

Vida was still reeling. 'He'd be court-martialled!'

'You'd think so, wouldn't you? The fact that he's doing it anyway suggests to me that someone, or something, is close to getting what they want.' The Doctor came away from the eyehole. 'Useless. I'll have to get out there and take off the tarp. You steer.'

'We're on the Thames in a tug boat.' She crossed to the wheel and gripped it with trembling hands. 'How far d'you think you're going to get?'

He crossed to the doorway. 'Doesn't take that long to get to the other side.'

'There'll be soldiers already heading us off!' She paused. 'So we've got to get to somewhere more public, haven't we? They can't just open fire in front of witnesses, can they? *Can* they?'

But her question hung in the air unanswered. The Doctor had gone.

NINE

Mickey had to admire Keisha's staying power. She was still rattling at the door with... well. He wanted to think it was superhuman strength, but since he was feeling kind of subhuman right now, it probably wasn't.

With a guilty twinge he half-wished it was Keisha who'd cleared off and Anne stuck in the bathroom. But she was Rose's mate and he wasn't about to let Rose down again.

'Just take it easy!' he yelled for the twentieth time. 'I ain't letting you go anywhere out in this state!' *Big words, Mickey*, he thought. But the truth was, he couldn't hold on much longer. Was there anywhere he could try to lock her inside, a cupboard or something? But no, it was the sort of furniture that came flat-packed with no proper instructions. It would fall apart in two seconds with someone like Keisha shut inside it –

But then the door handle finally slipped from his sweaty fingers as, with an almighty cry, Keisha rammed the door open. Make-up smeared, eyes red and narrowed, for a moment she was terrifying. He threw himself at her ankles, brought her down.

'Get off me!' she shrieked, kicking to be free.

'No way!' he shouted back, clinging on to her ankles. 'I let Anne go. No way am I letting you follow her.'

The phone started ringing shrilly as if in protest. They both ignored it till the answering machine kicked in. Then, as a female voice crackled out from the speaker, Keisha went suddenly rigid.

'It's your mum, love.' A long pause. 'Have you… have you seen him? Has Jay come to you?' She sounded as if she was trying not to cry.

Keisha was still holding herself dead still. Mickey was afraid she *was* dead for a moment, and cautiously let go of her legs.

'I'm coming down. Tomorrow.' Her voice was clipped now, trying so hard to hold it together. 'Because… he needs us. We've got to go to him, ain't we? Get to him before the feast.'

She stayed on the line for a few silent seconds. Then, with a click, she hung up. A chill went through Mickey as he clocked Keisha. She was holding herself as rigid as a corpse, her eyes wide and staring. A single fat tear had snaked through the black mush of her eyelashes and was dribbling down her cheek.

'You ain't heard from her in a while, have you?' he panted.

She shook her head a fraction. 'Not in years.' Then her eyes screwed up and the tears started in earnest.

Mickey stood up slowly, aching all over, watched as she curled into a ball. 'I'll make us some tea, yeah? Hot and sweet.' He walked wearily over to the kitchen. 'I think we could both use it.'

* * *

'That's her!' On the way to Waterloo, just as Rose was losing all hope of ever spotting Anne again, she glimpsed silver hair and tweed through the taxi window. The woman passed through a pool of streetlamp-orange before ducking down an alleyway close to the river.

Rose tapped the taxi driver on the shoulder. 'Can we get down there?'

'One-way system,' he grunted. 'Have to go round.'

Have to get out, then, she thought. 'Stop! I'm gonna be sick!'

The taxi driver braked hard. Rose threw open the passenger door and scrambled outside.

'Oi! What about my fare, you little –'

'I'll be back in a minute,' Rose yelled back, sprinting down the dark alley after Anne. 'I hope.'

The alley gave on to a posh little terrace of townhouses. Anne had cut across the road and through the parked cars. She was doglegging towards the river all right.

Rose forced herself to run faster, faster. 'Anne!' she cried, catching up now. 'Anne, wait! Listen to me!'

The woman suddenly turned. Rose's heart plummeted. It wasn't Anne at all, just some poor old lady, beside herself with terror.

'I don't have much money!' she said, clutching her little bag to her chest. 'Please leave me alone.'

Rose held up her hands. 'It's all right, I thought you –'

The woman changed tactic. 'Help,' she called. 'Someone help me!'

But her cries were drowned out by a chorus of screams beyond the courtyard.

'They're going to kill themselves!'

'Leave me alone!'

'Get back to your seats! If we tip over you'll end up in there with 'em!'

Still yelling 'sorry' over her shoulder, Rose followed the sound of the shouts. She ran out of the courtyard and dodged through the traffic on the main road, making for the thoroughfare beside the river. There was a big floating restaurant barge moored to her right, but so many diners had left their tables to stare out over the balcony rail that it was listing badly. A smaller crowd had gathered on a wharf jutting out over the river. As Rose ran to join them she could hear more cries:

'Why have you blocked off the bridges?'

'She's on that ship, she needs me!'

'We *have* to go!'

And when she reached the wharf she could see that, down on the tiny stretch of brown beach by the dark river, a dozen soldiers were struggling desperately with a ragtag crowd of men, women and children. They were holding them back, or trying to. Rose held her hand to her mouth as she saw one young boy, maybe eight or nine, break through the khaki barricade and hurl himself into the water. He was fished out by a soldier, but managed to break free and throw himself in again. 'My dad needs me!' he shouted. The soldier had to carry him out flailing and yelling, clutching him tight to stop him going in again. 'He needs my help! I have to get to him before the feast!'

The mad hoot of boat horns rose up from the river, like wild deranged animals in pain. Rose jostled past the onlookers and saw a river police patrol boat blocked by some kind of military vessel. Soldiers were jumping aboard. Rose thought she glimpsed huddled figures half-buried by blankets.

A man nudged her, conspiratorial. 'They say they've had dozens chucking themselves in,' he said. 'Just like lemmings, one after the other. Determined, they are.'

'She's still there!' sobbed a woman on the beach. 'I'm a good swimmer. You have to let me reach her. She's in the wreck of the *Ascendant*.'

'It's half a mile from here!' A soldier had his hands clamped on her shoulders. 'But even if it was right next door, you can't seriously –'

'It's true, she told me. I saw her!' The woman struggled in his grip. 'As plain as I'm seeing you!'

'They should've left that wreck at the bottom of the sea,' said another man, rousing Rose from her thoughts. 'It's cursed all right. They reckon this madness is carrying on up and down the river.'

Murmurs of agreement behind her. 'Anywhere they can get to the river, they're chucking themselves in. Anywhere that's not blocked off.'

Straight away, Rose realised that she would never see Anne again.

'It must be bad if they've got the marines in for it,' a girl in leathers agreed. 'Police can't cope.'

Or else they're not being given a chance to cope, thought Rose.

'It's sinful,' said an old man behind her. 'Suicide is a sin. These people should be ashamed.'

'They don't want to kill themselves,' Rose told him.

'Not in their right minds,' the know-all man agreed, as the soldiers finally brought the desperate crowd under control. 'Like those idiots at Christmas, ready to jump and end it all. Mass hysteria, that was.'

'No, I mean, these people aren't trying to kill themselves,' she insisted.

'Oh?' The man looked down at her sniffily. 'What makes *you* the expert?'

'Listen to them! This isn't about suicide. They just need to get to the people they love. People they thought they'd never see again. Wouldn't you do anything, *risk* anything, to reach someone that special? Even… even dying?'

He stared at her. 'You're a nutter, like they are!'

Rose opened her mouth but no words came out. *Jay is there*, a voice in her head was telling her. Just for a moment she felt a prickling at the back of her own mind, an urge to get down there and wade into the dark water. To find Jay, and help him. It would be so easy if she just –

The know-all nudged the person next to him. 'This one reckons them drowned sailors are sat on that tug boat, just waiting for visitors!'

There was another deranged chorus of hooting from along the river – from the other way this time – and fresh uproar from the restaurant barge as the clientele craned to see.

'That's the tug on the news,' someone cried. 'The one that towed the wreck!'

'It's ghosts! They've taken it over!'

'Who's riding it?'

Rose stared, dumbfounded. 'Oh. My. God.'

The Doctor was balancing precariously on the prow of the tug as it ploughed through the water, wrestling with a tarpaulin that was covering the cabin windows, yelling something at whoever was inside.

'New orders from Rear Admiral Crayshaw to all units,' one of the soldiers shouted. 'That boat's run a blockade and must be stopped.'

'We've got our hands full with this lot, sir,' cried another.

'Doctor!' Rose sprinted away from the wharf and back along the bank, racing to keep level with the tug. 'Look, the river's blocked up ahead! Police and soldiers.'

'Rose!' The Doctor looked across at her and waved cheerily. 'You all right? What are you doing here?'

'What am *I* doing?'

The Doctor had turned now to see both the river patrol boat and the ship with the soldiers, dead ahead. 'Don't like the look of them much.' He pointed to the restaurant barge. 'Hard to stop these things in a hurry. Need something to soften the impact.'

'You're joking.'

'Get everyone clear!'

'You're *not* joking,' she muttered, adrenalin sweeping her straight on to the deck of the barge. She jumped on to a prominent table for ten, almost slipped in the salad and kicked a lobster flying. 'Heads up, everybody,' she yelled over the resultant screams. 'Party of two on their way, and I don't think they've booked.'

* * *

Vida wondered if she would ever be able to prise her fingers loose from the ship's wheel. It was sinking in, now – bullets. Orders to kill. For a moment, going to pieces seemed like a great idea. Then a sense of outrage had overtaken her (sense? Ha!) and she in turn had overtaken every other boat on the river in the powerful tug, following the Doctor's frantic instructions about which way to spin the wheel.

But it wasn't just her fingers she could no longer feel; she was numb inside. How long could their luck hold? They were still running blind. The Doctor had freed a portion of the tarpaulin from the windows, but – Hang on, what was that he was shouting?

His head suddenly pushed back in through the tug's broken cabin window. 'Vida, does this thing do a handbrake turn?'

She sighed. 'Left or right?'

'Right.' He blinked. 'No protests? No argument?'

'Is there any point?'

The Doctor grinned. 'You *do* think I'm cute.'

She put on the brakes and spun the wheel, almost sent him tumbling into the Thames.

'Come on, everyone off!' Rose pointed to the tug, now speeding towards the restaurant on a collision course. 'Shift yourselves, then!'

Some of the diners had spotted the danger already, were already clearing out. But those at Rose's feet were just sat staring up at her in a mixture of shock and dismay. She grabbed a stuffed chicken breast from one woman's plate and chucked it off the barge. 'Well, go on!' she shouted. 'Fetch!'

* * *

'What the hell are we doing?' Vida asked, as the Doctor helped her scramble out through the broken window on to the prow of the boat. She hoped she didn't cut herself.

Then she saw the barge looming up ahead of them and decided that, hey, a cut or two might not be so bad as long as she could avoid the broken limbs, the multiple head injuries, the awful, gut-twisting smash of –

'Jump!' yelled the Doctor, yanking her off her feet.

'Come on, everyone *off*!' Rose yelled at the diners again. 'Quick and calm, yeah?' She was going to add some of that guff they told you in fire drills about not stopping for your belongings – but it was pointless, because she already had a full-blown stampede on her hands. The gangplank groaned under the weight of so many people clomping across it, both customers and the staff from below deck, brought up by the headwaiter with seconds to spare.

The tug was powering towards them in eerie silence, about to crush the nose of the barge against the river bank. The Doctor was poised at the prow, holding the hand of some slimline blonde – where did he find them?

More to the point, what was Rose doing just watching when that thing was about to smash this deck into matchwood?

Rose raced to the side of the barge and leaped desperately for dry land. There was an awesome, splintering crash behind her, and as she hit the ground it shook with the force of the collision. Mucky water rained down over her as she chanced a look back, saw the barge lurch and lift as it was crushed against the bank. The rending, scraping sound threatened to gouge out her eardrums.

'Doctor!' she yelled, her eyes fixing on the mangled mess of the two vessels. Both were sinking already, taking on water with alarming speed. There was no sign of him, and her insides felt gummed up with fear. Surely he couldn't be –

Then suddenly there he was, hauling himself over the side of the knackered barge with the blonde. She had a cut on her forehead, but otherwise they seemed OK.

For how much longer was another matter. Rose glanced behind her to find soldiers were charging up the street towards them. Quickly she jumped up and ran over to where the diners were milling about like lost lambs in search of a shepherd: Rose had decided to volunteer for the job.

'Ladies and gents, we're sorry for this disruption to your evening,' she announced, as poshly as poss. 'These soldiers you see approaching will gladly give the first twenty customers a full refund for your abandoned meal, together with generous compensation packages for any distress you may have experienced...'

Already, the canniest of the clientele were dashing off towards the soldiers, and it didn't take long for the rest to catch up. Soon they had formed an impenetrable scrum, all but blocking the street.

'Should keep the marines off our back for a minute or two,' Rose said, turning to the Doctor as he approached with the blonde. He was limping a bit, but smiley as ever. 'You all right?'

'Right as a trivet,' the Doctor replied. 'D'you think they

minded me barging in like that? Sorry.' He bustled them off ahead of him, heading back towards the courtyard. 'Vida Swann, meet Rose Tyler.'

'Hi. You must be the assistant he told me about.' The blonde smiled approvingly and looked up at the Doctor. 'You were right, I can see they come in *very* handy.'

Rose raised an eyebrow. 'Assistant, am I?'

'Well, not so much an assistant. More of a companion, really.' He clicked his fingers. 'Or associate – how about associate? No, sounds like something off *Crimewatch*. My aide? Sidekick?' He smiled at her. 'P'raps you're just Rose.'

'I like the sound of that better,' she agreed, smiling back.

'I don't like the sound of *those*,' said Vida. Rose listened too: sirens, getting closer. 'We're not out of this yet. This whole city will be after us now.'

'Oi! You, girlie!'

'Including that short, greasy bloke.' The Doctor turned to Rose. 'Why's he waving his fist at you?'

'Oh, God,' said Rose. 'It's my taxi driver. I had to do a runner and I didn't have the fare…'

'But this is perfect!' The Doctor welcomed the taxi driver with open arms. 'Can you take us to the headquarters of the European Office of Oceanic Research and Development?' He turned back to Rose with a confidential air. 'Vida works for them. Could be a useful temporary base of operations. We'll get Mickey and the others to meet us over there, I want to look at –'

The taxi driver finally found enough voice to butt in. 'You expect *me* to take you *anywhere*?'

'We can pay you, now! Pay you loads!' He nudged Vida. 'Flash some cash, then.'

Rose smiled at her sympathetically. 'He's a lousy date.'

Vida pulled out a twenty from her jacket pocket. 'And why do I get the feeling that now I've met him, I'm just going to go on paying?'

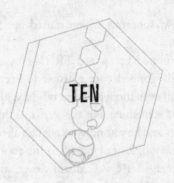

TEN

Leonard Huntley sat alone and disgruntled in the silent underground workshop. It was close to 11 p.m., and the systems had lowered the brilliant lights to a more sympathetic level. He'd been off duty for almost an hour, sat here in the sterile gloom, and still no sign of Crayshaw. No word of what had happened to the Doctor either, for that matter. Once the soldiers stamped out from the decontamination chamber empty-handed, it was as if no one dared even to discuss it.

Go home, he told himself. *He's obviously not coming. Our friendly neighbourhood intruder has led him a merry dance and worn the old boy out. Are you going to stick around all night?*

'Probably,' Huntley murmured, sighing. The suggestion from Crawshaw that he stay behind for a meeting had sounded to him suspiciously close to an order. Besides, there was no one at home expecting him. A few online chess players waiting for him to perform his next move, a half-empty bottle of wine and a TV dinner. All in all, the meeting with Crayshaw had seemed a far more exciting prospect – if it ever actually happened.

Then a low, sonorous whine started up. Someone was using the lift.

Huntley jumped up, wiped his clammy palms on his jumper. He'd agonised over whether to keep wearing the protective suit even though he was off-duty, just to prove his dedication or something. But the wretched thing made him sweat buckets and he was nervous enough already.

With a heavy industrial clunk the lift doors opened and Crayshaw emerged. He walked stiffly over, still wearing his dark glasses despite the gloomy lighting.

Huntley cleared his throat. 'Is everything all right, sir?'

Crayshaw said nothing, but kept walking towards him.

'I mean... has the intruder been caught yet?'

'Come with me, Huntley,' said Crayshaw. 'You will see what has been caught.' He walked straight past without a glance, heading for the door to the decon chamber.

Huntley frowned. Crayshaw had lingered there alone before following his marines back out again. Surely he'd sniffed out all the clues he was going to? 'Er, forgive me, sir, but I was wondering what it was you wished to discuss with me?' No response. 'Is it something to do with what the Doctor told me, or –'

'There's something I want you to see,' said Crayshaw, entering the access code.

The doors opened more smoothly than they had earlier. Some kind of sonic interference had completely scrambled the circuits, but luckily the systems boys had got on the case and fixed both outer and inner doors. You had to hand it to them...

No. On second thoughts, you didn't – they got enough credit around here as it was. But they hadn't been singled out by Crayshaw for the sharing of privileged information, had they? They weren't being shown into a shadowy decon chamber and the dank, filthy access corridor beyond in the dead of night. OK, fair enough, they probably wouldn't be jealous of that part, but even so…

Crayshaw led the way along the gloomy corridor, his step unerring and sure.

'Not been used for a while, this area,' Huntley observed. He was speaking to cover his unease, but the eerie echo only added to it. 'I suppose you'll order the remaining parts of the *Ascendant* to be taken down here in due course?'

'Why should I do that?' said Crayshaw quietly. 'You've made nothing of the other sections. This Doctor provided more information than the rest of you after only a few minutes.'

Huntley frowned. 'You know, I didn't mention this before, but… when the Doctor spoke to me, he did say something about *aliens*.'

'Aliens?'

'Aliens under the sea.' He forced a laugh, but it came out strangulated and high-pitched. 'High-tech sea monsters, I suppose. And I know that there have been all sorts of hoaxes and stunts concerning aliens visiting the Earth, but I firmly believe that there is a rational explanation for…'

As they came to the drainage chamber beneath the cargo lift, Huntley found the words drying in his throat. There were people clustered around the circular pool. They stood perfectly still. Ordinary people, of all colours – some suited, some scruffy, but all of them soaking wet, dripping on the grimy floor. Breathing slowly and heavily, in ragged unison.

'How – how did these people get here?' asked Huntley.

'The overspill pipeline.'

'The *what*?'

'It stretches from the river bed to the drainage pit.'

Huntley stared, bewildered, at the silent figures. 'How could they possibly get down there without drowning?'

Crayshaw smiled. 'They didn't.'

Now, with terror, Huntley recognised the awful grey pallor of the people in the chamber. He saw the red strafes on their cheeks and neck, the dull gleam in their eyes, as if moonlight had pooled there and turned slowly to stone. They looked like dead people, but –

'Is this some kind of sick joke?' he whispered. 'You think I can't see they're still alive?'

'Oh, yes,' said Crayshaw softly, raising his hands. 'They are full of life.'

'Will you stop speaking in riddles, and…'

Huntley stopped.

The old man had taken off his dark glasses. His eyes were huge, pale and shiny, like colossal pearls. His white skin began to unravel, melting and twisting like candlewax.

'We want you to join us for the feast, Huntley.' Crayshaw's voice was growing softer, more sibilant, almost feminine as his body dwindled and stooped, as the scarf slipped away.

Huntley screamed, staggered back, knocked into one of the silent onlookers – a mature lady in green tweeds. She toppled over; there was a splash. Huntley registered dimly that the pool was full almost to overflowing with dark water. A strong, salty smell flared his nostrils. There were further splashes as more and more of the ghoulish figures flopped into the water. He watched them, numb with fear. Not one rose again.

'This is their home now,' said the thing that had been Crayshaw. 'Their new life has begun. And so too will yours.'

'Let me go.' Huntley covered his face with both hands. 'I won't tell. I won't say anything to anyone.'

'But you know of anti-cellularisation. Of alien things.'

'No. No, I don't.'

'You are a solitary creature, Huntley. You may escape the feast. We cannot allow you to talk of this.'

'No, *please…*' Huntley babbled. 'I swear I don't believe in any of it.'

'Then let us arrange a demonstration.'

Through his fingers, Huntley glimpsed something sinewy and thick rise up before him. Grasping hands pulled him into the pool, and it was like falling into glass. The salty water poured into his mouth, thickening like old porridge, filling him like hunger. He glimpsed large silvery eyes staring into his own, felt a shooting pain at the back of his neck.

By then the blackness of the water was absolute, and he was lost.

Rose and the Doctor caught up in the back of the cab. Vida sat in the front seat. Her mobile phone was pressed to her ear, though she wasn't talking, just staring out of the window in silence. The taxi driver, mollified by cash, was playing country and western music. The duelling banjos and jaunty guitars made a bizarre soundtrack for the conversation.

'This big secret underground base you trashed,' said Rose, 'why was it built, then?'

The Doctor shrugged. 'Started off as usual Cold War paranoia, I expect, leading on from Q Whitehall.' He must have caught her blank look. 'You know, those deep tunnels for routeing power and communications between all the big government places, in case a nuclear war kicked off.' He kept his voice low, glanced over at the cab driver. 'Nowadays, with all this interest in the Earth from outer space… I'd say there were quite a few secret scientific bases in operation all over London.'

'All *under* it, you mean.' Rose looked down at her lap. 'I'm sorry I messed up. Didn't look after Anne like you told me.'

'It was no one's fault,' said the Doctor quietly. 'She'll have got her dearest wish by now. Gone to join her son.'

Rose nodded, though the thought hardly made her feel better. 'At least Mickey stopped Keish going after Jay.'

'Just as well. I've seen him.'

'Mickey?'

'Jay. Not some spooky see-through apparition. The *real* Jay. Or what he's become, anyway.' Rose shivered to see the haunted look on the Doctor's boyish face. 'S'pose he was holding up OK, considering he'd been subjected to some kind of alien vivisection. But I can't see him sending Keisha a postcard any time soon.'

'Will he be all right?'

The Doctor said nothing. The next song came on, some

mournful dirge about a mother losing her son.

'Why couldn't you take him with you?' she asked quietly.

'Funny story there. We were about to escape – very daringly, I might add – when a load of water tried to trap us and a pirate and a U-boat captain turned up out of nowhere and dragged him back down a 300-foot shaft into this big black puddle…'

'Oh. Is that all?' She wiped wetness from her eyes. 'Doctor, I so wanted to get to Jay. Swim to him, through the water. Once I saw him appear like that in the shop, I felt sure that he was there, under the river… The real him, you know. And I was sure that I could get to him. Whatever was in my way, I could overcome it.'

'But you didn't go.'

'No. No, I stopped myself.' She shrugged. 'I never even knew Jay that well. It was just a sort of crush.'

'You said that when he first appeared in the flat, he was speaking to Keisha. But then he noticed you too?'

'And he recognised me, yeah. That's when he asked me along to this feast thing like it just occurred to him. Like an afterthought.'

He nodded. 'How did that make you feel?'

'I was too busy being scared to death at the time to feel anything. But maybe I was a bit… I dunno, hurt.' She looked at him. ''Cause, well, he never took me seriously, did he? No one wants to feel like an afterthought…'

'That feeling may have saved your life.' The Doctor fidgeted in his seat. 'Are we there yet?'

Vida didn't turn round. 'Five minutes.'

Rose nudged the Doctor. 'What d'you mean, saved my life?'

'When the apparition of Jay came to you again… maybe a subconscious trace of that resentment made you wary. Stopped you trusting him absolutely, the way Keisha does. The way Anne trusted her son.' His angular features flashed in and out of streetlight and shadow. 'We trust the people we love to tell the truth. We trust them not to harm us. And something, some *force*, is trading on that.'

'But to do what?'

'I don't know.' He pulled something from his pocket, a little plastic bag full of water. 'That's what we've got to find out.'

The London premises of the European Office of Oceanic Research and Development were in Clerkenwell, a couple of floors in a tall, anonymous blackened-brick building. Vida waved off the cabbie with some extra notes and hurried up the steps to a large green door. She glanced all around before swiping her card in the thingy beside it.

'I don't think we were followed,' the Doctor offered.

Vida forced an awkward smile. 'Paranoid.' She led the way inside. It was all high ceilings, white corridors, deep-pile carpets – efficient and businesslike, but not too unfriendly.

'I've been trying to get hold of my boss,' Vida went on. 'Andrew Dolan, the man who swung me a place at Stanchion House, despite fierce opposition.' She brushed her hair from her face. 'Didn't know what fierce was, then.'

'Got a lab round here?' the Doctor asked abruptly.

'What? Oh, yes, we have several.'

'Show me the biggest. Biggest and shiniest!'

'All right.'

Rose found herself feeling sorry for Vida. She remembered how *she'd* felt when she'd found out just how many nightmares skulked in the shadows of her familiar world. She placed a hand on the woman's shoulder. 'Are you worried about him? Your boss, I mean?'

She looked grateful that Rose had bothered to ask. 'Crayshaw told me he'd talked with Andrew today. I haven't been able to get hold of Andrew since, not on any of his numbers. So what do I do now? Go to the police?'

'Wouldn't recommend it,' chirped the Doctor.

Vida put her hand to her head, scrunched up some hair as she thought. 'Will the navy high-ups be in on all this, d'you think? It was a Commodore Powers who put Crayshaw in charge of this investigation. If we went to him and told him what's been going on —'

'Even if they believed us, what could they do? They might hold an inquiry, wait a couple of months while they study the evidence…'

'While whatever's waiting to kick off gets right under way,' Rose added.

'Well, I should surely warn Kelper —'

'The powerful vice admiral from Norfolk,' the Doctor elucidated.

'— when he gets over here. He's meeting Crayshaw first thing, inspecting that wreck. And, oh joy, I'm supposed to be there with him.'

'I went on holiday to Norfolk, once,' Rose announced. 'Caravan in Cromer. Very flat.'

Vida sighed.

'Let's see what we can find to tell him before he arrives. Big shiny lab through here, is it?' The Doctor tried a set of large double doors but they were locked.

'Letting you in here without authorisation.' She shook her head as she entered another passcode. 'I'll get shot.'

'Cheer up. You've dodged the bullets so far tonight.'

Vida's glare was probably hard enough to open the lab doors unaided, but the Doctor gave them a helping hand.

'Oi, before you get all boy-with-a-train-set in there,' Rose said, producing her mobile, 'I'm just gonna call Mickey, see how him and Keisha –'

The Doctor nodded. 'Get him to drive her over here. Now.'

'Why?'

'I'm worried.'

'OK, but why are you –'

It was no good. The Doctor had already vanished inside. Vida followed him, shaking her head, and Rose knew exactly how she felt.

'So he wants us over there on the double, does he?' said Mickey, jotting down the address, the phone warm against his ear. He glanced over at Keisha, still sleeping on the sofa. 'Nice to feel wanted for once.'

'Is Keisha OK?'

'I think she is now. She was going crazy, but then her mum called.'

'But her mum's a cow!'

'Can't be all bad. When Keisha heard her mum's voice it stopped her fit. She's resting now.'

'Sorry I had to leave the two of you alone, when you don't… well, you know. You're so sweet, though, doing that for me.'

'Well, she's your mate, ain't she?' He paused. Maybe he should just come out and say it. Tell Rose the real reason for the awkwardness, the bad feeling –

'Anyway, it's not just the Doctor – I want you here too, Mickey. I need someone to bunk off with.'

'You what?'

'I mean, I think I'm in for a chemistry lesson. And I always used to bunk off Science.'

'Bad girl.'

'You love it.'

He smiled. 'I'll get there as soon as I can. See you soon, yeah?'

'Yeah.'

She rang off. Mickey stared at the phone for a full minute before he shoved it back in his pocket and gently shook Keisha awake.

Her green eyes snapped open and she tensed, sat bolt upright.

'It's OK,' said Mickey. 'It's only me.'

She relaxed, but just a little, something unsteady in her gaze. 'It was me what woke you up last time, wasn't it?'

Mickey looked away. 'We'd better get going. Rose and the Doctor want us to go and see them.'

'But Mum's coming!'

'You can leave her a note or something.' He hesitated. 'Look, I know you haven't seen her in years… but she won't be here before morning, will she? And I'll have brought you back home by then.'

She looked at him. 'My personal chauffeur?'

He shrugged. 'S'all right.'

'Wow,' she said. 'You really *are* feeling guilty, aren't you?'

He turned angrily away, but she jumped up and put her hand on his shoulder. 'No, wait. I'm sorry.'

Her hand felt cold through his shirt. 'Whatever.'

'I was out of order. I'm just...' She crossed round to stand in front of him, and he could see fresh tears in her eyes. 'I'm just so, so scared, Mickey. I've never had much, and Jay was so precious to me and now... now he's gone and Mum says she's coming down and... what if I mess this up?' She crumpled into his arms. 'Mickey, I drive people away and I just mess everything up.'

He stood there while Keisha held on to him, pressing her wet face against his neck. But all he could really feel was the heat in his ear from the mobile.

'We'd better go.' He patted her back, then stepped carefully away. 'We'll talk about it more in the car, yeah?'

She wiped her nose on a wet tissue and forced a tiny smile. 'Yeah.'

They crossed to the front door and left.

Beside the sofa, in her abandoned handbag, Anne's mobile phone bleeped an electronic 'Greensleeves' as somebody called. The tune played on, plaintively, in the empty flat.

Rose slipped the phone back into her pocket and wandered inside the big oceanic research lab. It was shiny all right, white and modern, well kitted out. The Doctor had got busy, assembling stands and beakers and Bunsens on a bench, together with loads of stuff she didn't recognise.

Vida was watching him warily. 'Help yourself, by the way.'

The Doctor flashed her a dazzling grin. 'I will, ta. Hey, here's Rose! Hello, Rose. Keisha on her way in?'

'She will be.' Rose stared at some charts on the wall, which showed loads of tiny dotted paths against a deep-blue background. 'What d'you do here, Vida? I mean, what do you research in the ocean and that?'

'We analyse the sea's constituent elements over time.' Vida seemed to brighten a little – perhaps because she was in safer, more familiar waters now. 'Our research is pretty cutting edge, actually. We help establish global ocean and deep basin circulation patterns, identify biogeochemical processes in the ocean, explore the transport pathways of spilled materials...'

Rose turned up her nose. 'Takes all the fun out of swimming in it, I'll bet.'

'You might not want to swim if you knew what was in the water.'

'What... sharks and things?'

'I was thinking on a less visible level.'

'Always the most dangerous,' the Doctor agreed, splashing some drops from his bag of water into a glass flask.

'That bit about spilled materials,' said Rose. 'D'you mean, you check how pollution spreads in the water and stuff?'

'Exactly. Identifying and measuring both natural and pollutant chemicals in the ocean.' Vida nodded. 'That's one of the best ways of utilising our findings here.'

'But there are others,' said the Doctor. He had fixed his flask to the stand and was now riffling through some jars in a fume cabinet. 'You use chemical tracers to study the spread of these pollutants, right?'

'Sometimes.'

'And you release them from ships like the *Ascendant*. Sharing your findings with the military.'

Vida nodded slowly. 'We're a civil organisation. But the US military have sponsored certain experiments. For this one we were using newly developed tracers – subatomic filaments in an aqueous base. Tiny organic transmitters and receivers, they can tell us wherever they are in the ocean. Harmless to all life of course –'

The Doctor clicked his tongue. 'In theory.'

'And in practice.'

'But practice doesn't always make perfect.' He crossed back to the bench with a few jars, widened his eyes at her. 'Now, it seems to me you have a big American back admiral in your rear pocket – or something. Funny he should take such an interest in your pollution research.' He sniffed one of the jars and recoiled. 'Then again, depends on the payoff. Once you can accurately predict the spread of certain chemical agents in the water, well, the sky's the limit. Or the ocean is, anyway.' He poured some of the jar's contents into his flask. 'You can flood an enemy's harbour or fishing grounds with those tiny subatomic filaments – in a suitable chemical solution, of course – and then all you need's an activation signal…'

'And what would that be activating, then?' Rose queried.

'Oh, what d'you reckon, Vida? A corrosive element to

destroy a fleet of ships or a berth of submarines?' suggested the Doctor cheerily. 'Biological agents programmed to wipe out certain indigenous fish, forcing a nation into unfair fishing agreements…'

Vida eyed him coldly. 'What are you talking about?'

The Doctor's cheery look had soured too. 'Come on, don't say the possibilities haven't occurred to you. Or to Kelper.'

'Any theoretical research has a lot of potential applications.'

'I know,' he said darkly, buzzing the sonic screwdriver at the water in the flask. 'I've seen some of them in action. In just a few years from now.'

'Who *are* you?' Vida stared at him, then at Rose. 'Who do you work for?'

'If anything we work *against*,' said Rose. 'Against bad people. Monsters.'

'Well, Doctor whoever-you-are with your resourceful teenaged assistant, I'm sorry if my work makes me a monster in your eyes, but I'm really not in the mood for a personal attack right now.'

Rose realised how her words had come out. 'Look, I didn't mean –'

'No, don't bother.' Vida pushed out her chin defiantly, but her lip was quivering just a fraction. 'I'm letting you abuse my facilities against my better judgement, but I'm damned if I'll let you start abusing *me*. You two may stroll through days like these with happy abandon, but I am seriously stumbling here. So just… just get on with whatever it is you're doing to that water, Doctor, so we can start getting our heads round some answers.'

'Good idea,' said the Doctor smoothly. Then he nodded to himself as he stirred the syrupy liquid in the beaker with the screwdriver and dabbed some of it on to a microscope slide. 'And you're right, of course. Any scientific technique can become a weapon where there's a will for it. Just take hydrogen-fused anti-cellularisation…'

'What?'

'It reworks matter at an atomic level. Metal, machinery, flesh – all fair game. Somebody's used it on the *Ascendant* – and its crew.'

Vida sounded timid and fragile: 'And you say it's aliens doing this?'

He nodded. 'Maybe they were after your super-duper new tracer. You know, the Subatomic Filaments in the Aqueous Chemical Base, TM.'

'Why?' wondered Rose. 'You think they want to check the spread of something in the ocean?'

'The filaments transmit. Maybe they want to use them somehow.'

'But if they're so advanced they can mess about with atoms –'

'Advanced is one of those funny words, Rose,' the Doctor told her. 'Some things come easier to some species than others. I mean, you couldn't spin a web, but does that make you less advanced than a spider?' He turned back to Vida. 'You say you've never had days like these, but I reckon you've flirted with them. Back on the tug when I mentioned there being something in the water, that hit a nerve, didn't it? You and Andrew found out something. What?'

Vida, apparently rumbled, sat down heavily on a lab stool. 'We sent survey boats out into the North Sea around where the *Ascendant* sank. Took samples from the water to see if the new tracers had been released before the ship went down.' She paused for a few moments, as if transfixed by the bubbling liquid. 'We studied the geochemistry of the samples. No sign of the tracers. But within a three-mile radius of the sinking, we found elements unheard of on Earth. Like salts and proteins, but completely unlike any previously discovered. The coding was…' She trailed off, shaking her head. 'It can only be described as alien.'

'A by-product of the fusion process?' mused the Doctor, switching on a weird-looking microscope on the next bench. 'Or something else?'

'What is that you're testing, anyway?' asked Rose.

'Water from the drainage pit beneath the cargo lift shaft. Smelled a bit fishy to me, so I…' He noticed Vida look away, bite her lip. 'Oh, big fat reaction again, Vida.'

'Andrew… my boss. When the wreck of the *Ascendant* was taken to Stanchion House, Crayshaw started being super-obstructive. We wondered what he might be hiding, especially after the weird water we found. So Andrew managed to get hold of the plans for Stanchion House – the underground part, I mean. We wanted to know if there was any other way of getting to the wreckage – seemed about the only way we might find out what happened to our tracers.'

'Sneaky,' said the Doctor approvingly, as he slipped the microscope slide into place. 'What did you learn?'

'That the drainage pit was extended two months ago, by

around 500 feet. Shortly before the wreck was recovered.' Vida dabbed at the cut on her forehead. 'It was about the first thing Crayshaw did after he was assigned to manage the affair.'

'But why bother?' said Rose.

'We couldn't ask him, could we?' Vida sounded bitter. 'All top secret, we weren't supposed to know. Which is why we were trying to arrange for Kelper to perform a surprise inspection ahead of the one he'd agreed with Crayshaw. Try to get past all the bull and find the truth.'

'Come on, the truth's obvious, isn't it?' The Doctor was squinting through the eyepiece of the microscope. 'Once the new extension was built, that drainage pit was flooded. He's been getting things ready. Building a little home from home.'

'Then that's where Jay's being held,' Rose realised. 'And Peter.'

'And quite possibly the rest of the crew, too. But what about the likes of Anne? Why would they want relatives and friends?' The Doctor looked up crossly. 'D'you reckon Mickey's got lost? Where's that Keisha?'

'Why d'you need her?'

'To see if I can find the same things in her that are in this water sample,' he said, looking meaningfully at Vida. 'Alien salts and proteins.'

Vida nodded, a look of resignation on her face as she crossed to a sort of high-tech fridge in the corner. 'I'll fetch one of the North Sea samples for comparison.'

'And some hypodermics while you're at it. That OK?'

'We should have some somewhere.'

'So we're fighting dirty water,' Rose summed up. 'That's impressive.'

'We're fighting something that has an *affinity* with water,' he retorted. 'Something that can harness it, adapt it to suit a purpose – even borrow it from human beings in the vicinity.'

'What?'

'Well, that's pretty much all you are, you humans – big bags of water.'

'I remember you saying something like that.'

'Brain – 70 per cent water. Lungs – almost 90 per cent water. Blood – 83 per cent. Your cells are full of the stuff.'

'$H_2Omigod$,' said Rose, a tingle running through her. 'Those soldiers, Mickey, the newsagent – all just dehydrating whenever a "ghost" comes near. That's how these things project themselves.'

'I'm going to ignore the "you humans" bit,' Vida announced, as she passed the Doctor the promised phial and syringes. 'And I'd *like* to ignore that stuff about hydrogen fusion you spouted. But with two atoms of hydrogen available in every water molecule, that's a lot of potential for "anti-cellularisation".'

'You're right there.'

'Incredible to think that an alien life form can adapt to take such advantage of its environment…' Vida buried her face in her hands. 'Oh, God, listen to me. I'm starting to swallow this whole mad story.'

'Well, water's generally easy to swallow,' said the Doctor, breaking the syringe from its plastic wrapper. 'Must be why they say drowning's a good way to go.'

'Could that tie in with this stuff about the feast of the drowned, then?' Rose ventured. 'They've swallowed this stuff in the water?' The Doctor shrugged. 'Hang on, though, how come you think it might have got into Keisha?'

The Doctor raised one shoulder. 'Just a hunch. It's probably in your blood too, of course. Come on, roll up your sleeve. Let's have a splash of the old red stuff.'

'Oh, nice.' Rose felt a buzz against her hip. 'Saved by the SMS. Hang on.' She pulled out her phone. 'Mickey's outside with Keisha. Waiting to be let in.'

The Doctor turned to his beaker of water. 'I wonder how long this force has been waiting in the North Sea... and what decided it to let itself in now.' He looked up at her. 'Just what does it want?'

Rose nodded slowly. 'And how long have we got to stop it?'

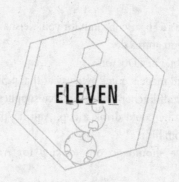

ELEVEN

Mickey sat spinning himself round in a swivel chair in the boss's office, half a mug of cold coffee in his hands. Rose had perched herself on the edge of a desk, and was looking out of the window at the dark street below.

'Listen to those sirens,' she said, as the sound carried distantly.

'They've been going all night.' Mickey rubbed his eyes. 'And so have we. You look knackered.'

'Thanks!' Rose retorted with a smile.

'It's a shame, though, isn't it?' He stopped swivelling long enough to look at her. 'We only ever get to spend a bit of time together when weird stuff is going on.'

She got up from the desk, changed the subject. 'I feel useless, just sitting here.'

'How d'you think *I* feel? All I'm good for is playing chauffeur for your mate!'

As soon as they had turned up, the Doctor had whisked Keisha off for 'tests'. He'd already taken a bit of blood from Rose. Now he cracked open a new syringe with an apologetic smile. 'There's a sugar cube in it for you, Keisha.'

'What're you gonna do?'

'It's all right. I'm a Doctor.'

Mickey had made a quick getaway at that point. Found his way to the staff kitchen and the coffee supplies, and a quiet office where he could drink a cup. And happily, Rose had decided to join him.

'Maybe we should go out looking for Anne,' Mickey suggested.

'I don't think we stand a big chance of finding her.'

'We don't know that, do we?'

She looked at him sympathetically. 'I feel bad about it too, you know.'

Mickey looked away. 'Wasn't you who let her go, was it?'

'It wasn't your fault. You were sick.' She pointed to his coffee. 'And you shouldn't be drinking that. It makes you wee more, and you're trying to put water back.'

'Can't do anything right tonight, can I?'

'Cheer up.' She crossed back to the window. 'Long way to go till this night's over.'

Just then the door opened and in came Vida Swann. Mickey had met her briefly on his way in. She was proper fit for an older woman, though right now she was looking as worn and crumpled as the lab coat she wore. One sleeve was rolled up, and she was dabbing at her arm with a piece of cotton wool.

'Spiked you too, did he?' Mickey asked.

'I'm the control, apparently.' She yawned. 'The Doctor says you're good with computers, Mickey.'

He brightened a little. 'I'm not bad.'

'Says you have experience of military websites.'

He couldn't help a small smile. 'A bit.'

'Why are you asking about computers?' Rose wondered.

'The Doctor wants me to trawl through naval personnel records for the crew of the *Ascendant*,' Vida explained. 'To see if they had anything in common, some link that might mark them out.'

'That could take ages,' said Mickey.

'Which is why the Doctor said you'd help me.' Vida sat at the next desk, in front of a flash-looking computer. It chimed loudly as it was stirred into start-up. 'I've got limited access to certain areas of the site, but we need to get into the service files.'

He nodded, started up the computer in front of him. 'Yeah, OK. Should be cool.'

'Well, that's nice for you two,' said Rose, heading towards the door.

'You could give us a hand,' Mickey suggested.

She turned and smiled at him sweetly. 'Make some more coffee for you, maybe?'

He grinned. 'If you're offering...'

'I'll see ya.' Rose waved goodbye and out she went.

Mickey watched her go, sighed, and got to work.

Rose found the Doctor was shining a torch thing into Keisha's eyes. Keisha was sat on a stool looking nervous; the small mountain of chemistry equipment on the bench beside her couldn't be helping.

'Dr Frankenstein, is it?' Rose said.

'Nah, just a talented amateur,' the Doctor replied. 'Though you should see what I've been doing with that water sample.' He put on a spooky, mad-scientist voice. 'It's alive!'

'Am *I* gonna live, then?' Keisha asked, reminding him of her existence through a forced smile.

The Doctor looked over at Rose. 'You know, it's just as I thought. Like you, she's got alien matter in her blood.'

Keisha frowned. '*What?*'

'Shh,' the Doctor told her, and turned back to Rose. 'She's got little specks of white in her eyes, too. Very odd.'

'*She* has a name, you know.' Rose rushed over and crouched beside Keisha, held her hand. 'Your bedside manner stinks.'

Keisha looked anxiously at her friend. 'What's he on about, *aliens*? He's saying there's stuff inside me, even in my eyes!'

The Doctor pouted. 'And you know, I've seen something like it before.'

'Where?'

'In oysters.'

'He's barking!' Keisha complained.

'Shhh,' the Doctor said again. 'An oyster doesn't make a pearl for fun, you know. It happens when it's in pain. It sometimes gets a bit of dirt or whatever stuck between its mantle and its shell, like you might get a splinter in your finger. But because oysters aren't so good with tweezers, they try to bury it, stop it hurting. Secrete this stuff that hardens over the splinter, layer after layer.' He nodded. 'We're starting to see something similar here.'

'You saying my eyes are turning into pearls?'

'Only that there's been some trauma in the area of the optic nerve and your body – tanked up with the weird alien proteins in your blood – is trying to soothe it, to cover it up.' He gave her a steady look. 'But if given the chance, the effect *can* get out of control. So you have to stop believing in that vision of Jay.'

Keisha reacted as if she'd been slapped. 'What are you on about? I *must* get to him.'

He took both of her hands, tenderly. 'No, Keisha, you mustn't. Because it's not Jay.'

'It is!' She snatched her hands away, looked imploringly at Rose. 'What's he *on* about?'

'I imagine it's gone to work on your brain cells too, making you more susceptible to suggestion,' the Doctor concluded. 'Hard to tell for sure without taking a sample from the brain stem.'

'Get off me!' Keish jumped up, and her chair went clattering across the shiny floor.

'Go easy on her, Doctor.'

So the Doctor marched up to Rose instead, and shone his torch in her eye. 'Hmm, thought so. We've got the same process going on here… though the damage is less advanced.' He patted her on the shoulder, consolingly. 'The alien cells are loads more concentrated in Keisha. She's awash with the stuff.'

'Are you trying to scare me on purpose?' said Keisha.

'I imagine it's because her feelings for Jay run so much deeper than yours, Rose. Must make it easier for the stuff to get into her body chemistry.' He smiled, a blown-away sort of smile. 'They say you can't measure emotions with science.

Well, this stuff makes it easy! Your two samples give us a chemical measure of the difference between heartbreak and mild regret. Isn't that amazing? It's wonderful!'

Rose felt Keisha's eyes on her and blushed. 'I don't just feel mild regret about Jay, Doctor!'

'The proof's in your blood,' he said, oblivious to her embarrassment. 'What worries me is the way it got there. Airborne infection? Mental projection? And then there's the other big question. Those soldiers on the bridge got drunk dry when there was a whole river underneath them going begging. Why?' He gasped. Then sucked in his cheeks. Then blew out a deep breath and clicked his fingers. 'Mental *and* airborne! This is about pheromones. Pheromones taken to the max!'

'We bunked off science, OK?'

'Pheromones – a kind of communication through chemicals,' he explained. 'Little airborne signals just waiting for the right receivers. Did you know a male moth can detect the spray of a ripe lady moth up to a mile away. He gets the signal, drops whatever he's doing and goes off to chat her up.'

'I'm so happy for Mr and Mrs Moth. What are you on about?'

'These water-based life forms can dip into the human body and brain, right? You two are living proof of that.' He glanced at Keisha. 'And when Jay appeared to you, you saw him just as he used to be. You believed absolutely it was him, despite all the evidence screaming that it couldn't be.'

'It *was* him,' Keisha insisted, her voice wavering.

'And yet Mickey, who's never met Jay, couldn't see him at

all.' He looked at Rose. 'Just as we couldn't see Anne's son on the bridge, when to her he was clear as day.'

Rose sighed. 'Go on, then, Sherlock. What's this got to do with pheromones?'

'What if these water-creatures collected sensory information from Jay, about himself and the people that lived in his memory, and *exported* it?'

'What, you mean like opening a computer file and saving it as something else so another program can read it?'

'Exactly. They exported it as a bundle of alien pheromones – *Essence of Jay*, from Calvin Klein – and transmitted it through human cell-water.' He laughed, shook his head in wonderment. 'Alien pheromones that can pass through aquatic molecules like nobody's business. Water in the body, in the breath, in the air... Passing at the speed of thought from person to person to person, through villages, towns and cities ...'

'Like those filaments in Vida's chemical tracers,' Rose realised, 'spreading and circulating through the ocean...'

'An ocean of humanity,' the Doctor agreed. 'Carrying information you can trace – or weapons you can trigger. And these creatures trigger *their* weapon when they finally find someone they recognise from Jay's memory, someone who responds to the pheromones. With a chemical push, they help the victim make sense of the signals to create the apparition and – wallop! You're a believer. You're caught. Easy when you know how.'

Rose struggled to take it in. 'Doesn't sound the easiest way to catch someone.'

'Spinning a web looks complicated to anyone other than the spider,' he retorted. 'A spider just gets on with it, because it's what a spider does.'

'But the power they'd need to do that…'

'Makes them very, very dangerous.' The Doctor clicked his tongue. 'Cheer up. It's all guesswork, I could be totally wrong. Who cares? Doesn't really matter at the end of the day. What does matter is – why? Why reel in the crew's loved ones like this?'

'Will you just shut up?' Keisha stared at him, her eyes big and shiny with tears. 'You make it all sound like… like it's just a stupid crossword clue or something! Jay's in trouble, he *needs* me. My mum's seen him too, and when she gets here…'

'Your mum's coming?' The Doctor rounded on her. 'You said back at your flat that she wouldn't care if he was dead, that she'd abandoned you.'

'Well, I was wrong! She's coming over tomorrow. She told me.'

'Must have been a bit of a shock, hearing from her after so long.' He glanced back at Rose. 'Probably saved her life, a jolt to the consciousness like that. Her natural emotions overcame the exaggerated ones stirred up by the pheromones. But even now they're starting to take control again.'

'Stop it!' Keisha shouted. 'We're gonna be a family again. Me, Jay, Mum. *All* of us.' Her face twisting with tears, she turned and stormed out of the lab.

Rose began to follow her, but the Doctor grabbed hold of her arm. 'You see? She can't think straight. That alien stuff won't let her. She'll go on believing what it wants her to until it's too late.'

'She's still my mate. I'd better see if she's all right.' She paused. 'What are you going to do?'

'I'm going to keep testing that water… I'm going to see if Vida and Mickey dig up something on the crew…' He unrolled a large sheet of paper on one of the lab benches. 'And I think I'd better take a look at Vida's plans of the underground citadel.'

Rose raised her eyebrows. 'What are you looking for?'

He gave her his craftiest, most feline grin. 'A back door.'

'Happy hunting, then.' She waved and went off after Keisha.

But on her way out she noticed a small puddle on the tiled floor. For a moment her heart skipped. Then she looked up and saw a discoloured patch on a ceiling tile. A little bead of water dripped down from it.

She blew out a shaky breath. What was she like? It was just a leaky pipe or something.

As she went off after Keisha, she didn't see the puddle swell and bubble out from the tiles and start to flow inside the lab.

The screen was blurring in front of Vida's eyes, and she forced herself to concentrate. It was late, and the day seemed to have gone on for ever. She wished she was somewhere else, far away and sunny, doing the things it was fun to stay up all night doing. But not sleeping. She couldn't imagine ever wanting to fall asleep again, now she knew what waited in the dark.

The bottom had fallen out of her life. She had told the

Doctor just about every secret she knew, even shown him the new transmitting tracers which only a handful of people were supposed to know about. The Doctor had grinned and called them quaint. Vida felt like calling him one or two words too.

She was hanging out for a hug right now. Where the hell was Andrew?

'Found anything weird yet?' asked Mickey through a yawn.

'Apart from the way I'm sitting here with a complete stranger riffling through confidential files for clues as to why an alien intelligence might have sunk a frigate? No.'

'Only asking,' he muttered.

'A vice admiral is showing up in a few hours. If Andrew doesn't put in an appearance soon – he's my boss – I'll have to go solo and...' She slumped forwards, pushing her head against the cool glass of the monitor screen. 'What do I tell him? What the hell do I tell him? He's been putting all the secrecy around the wreck down to some internal cover-up, trying to stop high-up heads rolling.'

'Tell him the truth – that it's down to aliens.'

'It's one thing finding unidentified organisms in sea water. It's another finding them in the bodies of senior naval personnel.' She raised her head wearily. 'Besides, Crayshaw would rip a story like that into pieces, and I'd soon follow.'

'Crayshaw.' Mickey flung his arms out in a big stretch. 'He's the big man, calling the shots, yeah?'

'Skinny little man, more like.' Vida clicked on her fiftieth file – soon to be, she was sure, her fiftieth dead-end. 'Rear Admiral John Anthony Crayshaw. What about him?'

'Bit past it, don't you reckon? Who put him in charge?'

'Good question.' Vida shrugged. 'We made some inquiries, trying to go above his head. But no one seemed quite sure how he was selected. We were referred to a Commodore Powers, who was meant to be handling the inquiry into the *Ascendant*, but he never got back to us. Suppose he deferred to the higher rank.'

Mickey sat up straighter in his seat. 'That's Commodore James Powers, age forty-five, on the Directorate of Navy Plans at Whitehall, yeah?'

'Yeah. He's responsible for deploying those soldiers around Stanchion House, securing the area around the wreck.' Vida looked over to his desk. 'Why have you brought his file up?'

'Why not? We're getting nowhere with the small fry, may as well check out the big geezers.' His lips moved a little as he read. Then he frowned. 'Wonder if this is why they chose Powers for the job. He was on a tub that went down in the North Sea too.'

'Or the German Ocean, as Crayshaw calls it,' she scoffed as she crossed to join Mickey. 'I know he's old, but the North Sea hasn't been called that since for ever…' Looking over his shoulder, she checked out the file. 'Three years ago, HMS *Lancer*.'

'I don't remember hearing about it.'

'Smaller ship, crew of just thirty. Easier to hush up.' She read on. 'Powers was the only survivor, picked up in a lifeboat…'

'And took a lot of time off work by the look of it,' said Mickey. 'Extended sick leave.' He clicked on another area of the website, brought up another submenu. 'What about Crayshaw, wonder if *he* ever sank?'

Vida waited while he worked to bring up the old git's record.

'Funny. He ain't here.'

'He's a rear admiral. The file's probably restricted.'

'I'll search the whole site, see if anything comes up,' Mickey announced.

'OK.' Vida crossed back to her chair and slumped in it, closed her eyes, let the drowsy hum of the computers drag her into a daze.

'Oh. My. God. It came up.'

'What did?' she said a little grouchily.

'*How* long since they stopped calling the North Sea the German Ocean?'

'I don't know. Some time in the nineteenth century?'

'Well, old habits die hard. And he's been around long enough to get a few.'

Reluctantly she opened her eyes. 'What are you on about?'

'The only place I can find any mention of this John Anthony Crayshaw bloke is in the naval history section. He was fifty-five and his ship, the *Ballantine*, went down in a storm. And what d'you know – that was in the North Sea.' Mickey turned to look at her, grave-faced. 'In 1759.'

For a few moments all she could do was stare at him. 'That's crazy. I mean, I know he looks old, but getting on for his 250th birthday?'

Mickey shrugged. 'You're probably right. Probably just a weird coincidence.'

'I mean, it's not very likely that Powers picked a footnote from naval history to head up this inquiry and give him control over the military presence around Stanchion House, is it?'

'Right. Let's not get carried away.'

'No. Don't want to look stupid.'

'Nah.'

They sat in silence for about two seconds before jumping up from their seats and sprinting to tell the Doctor.

The Doctor caught a flash of movement in the corner of his eye, looked up from the plans. No sign of anything.

Then he realised the water he'd been analysing had vanished. The beaker was empty.

A faint seaside whiff caught in his nostrils.

'You're here, aren't you?' he said aloud, staring round. The room seemed empty. Then he saw the sink was almost full, and yet he'd run no –

The water jumped out of the sink like a living thing, struck his face as cold and hard as glass. He fell backwards against the lab bench, sent it screeching across the floor, collapsed to his knees. He couldn't breathe. The water was squeezing up his nose, through his lips, forcing its way into his eyes.

Revenge, he thought. *It's testing me just like I tested it.*

'No,' he said, spitting the word out into the water, forcing himself to stay calm. 'Get out.'

But the pressure was rising in his head. It was like tasting history, old, sour and salty on his tongue. He felt the growth of slow centuries, ancient knowledge amassing somewhere beyond the tip of his mind, an insistent feeling that the time was drawing near. Time for the feast…

Screaming soundlessly, the Doctor fought to cling on to consciousness as the alien fluid stepped up its attack.

Rose found Keisha further down the corridor. 'Keish,' she said gently, 'are you OK?'

'Yeah. Great.' Keisha turned around, her face hard and tear-stained. 'D'you remember Old Scary?'

'Course I do,' said Rose, puzzled. Old Scary was a weird nutter who used to tramp around the estate when she and Keisha were kids.

'He used to scare the hell out of me,' Keisha went on, 'dragging that shopping trolley full of junk around, yelling bits of old poems and other stuff. Remember? He'd show up in my nightmares sometimes, shouting about doom and destruction and the end of the world.'

Rose nodded. 'He used to scare me too.'

'Well, next to your Doctor, Old Scary's a cuddly teddy bear, ain't he?'

'Oh, come on!'

'Rose, how can you bear him? In, like, five minutes he's scared me more than I've ever been scared in my whole life. He's poked me about, told me my eyes are gonna be oysters, I'm turning into an alien and my brain's being messed with.' She nodded, her lip curling. 'Oh yeah, and he's shown me that my so-called mate couldn't care less if my brother's dead.'

'I do care!'

'You *mildly regret* it, he said.'

'It's not like that…' Rose tried to take her hand, but Keisha snatched it away. 'Look, I know you're upset but –'

'Course you know. Rose Tyler knows everything these days since she's taken up with her cute little weirdo.' Rose caught the glitter of pearl in Keisha's eyes. 'Well, here's something you *don't* know.'

'Keisha –'

'The minute you went off travelling, right, Mickey came sniffing round me.'

Rose was floored. She stared at her old mate. 'He never.'

'He did. He came round and he tried it on.'

'Yeah?' She folded her arms. 'And what did *you* do?'

Keisha's face clouded, she looked away. And in that moment Rose realised she already knew, and it was like someone kicking her inside.

'What do you care anyway?' said Keisha, suddenly back on the attack. 'You just went off for a whole year with not a word, not a call. Not even a text, for God's sake!'

'I thought I was coming back!' she shouted.

'And when you do get back, you *still* don't bother calling, do you?'

'Don't twist this round! You've just told me that *you*…' Rose felt her throat burning. 'That you and him…'

'Hey, hey, what's happening?'

Rose turned to find Mickey rushing down the corridor, Vida just behind him. He looked worried.

With good reason…

'How could you, Mickey?' she said quietly. She said it again, lost for any other words: 'How could you?'

Straight off, he knew what she was talking about. She saw the look on his face. Guilt, dismay, no fight in him.

'It's true, then,' she said.

It was weird. Suddenly, the monsters, the alien plan, that was all background stuff. All she could think about was the horrible *wrongness* of Mickey being with one of her best mates.

Until the monsters came back.

Suddenly water flooded down from the ceiling, a ton of it, drenching them all. Rose was knocked to her knees, and Vida let out a shriek of surprise. Then the water seemed to thicken, and suddenly three threatening figures stood in the corridor.

One looked like a pirate. One looked like he'd parked his sub outside. The third was a woman in Victorian dress, who might once have been pretty. Now, like the others, her face was blotchy and bloated, eyes like enormous bulging pearls.

Keisha was already screaming. Mickey started forwards to tackle the pirate, but was knocked back by a powerful blow. 'No!' Rose shouted as he crashed against the wall and his eyes flickered shut. She grabbed the U-boat captain by the shoulders, and cringed as something cold and lumpy squished beneath her hands. That wrong-footed her, and he was able to shrug her off quite casually, sending her sprawling into Keisha. At least it shut up the screaming.

The Victorian girl and the pirate were already making for Vida, their backs hunched, arms outstretched. The U-boat man was following.

'Run, Vida!' Rose shouted. 'It's you they want!'

Vida had just twigged and was running back the same way she had come. As Rose scrambled up she saw the Victorian girl melt away, clothes and everything. A wave of water surged along the corridor, broke over Vida's ankles, swept past her.

And suddenly the Victorian girl blinked back into existence, arms wide open, eyes bulging and blank. Vida gasped, tried to duck aside, but the girl snatched her up, held her tight despite her struggles. Rose sprinted over to help her, but the pirate turned and lashed out with the back of his hand. She parried the blow with both hands, gripped on to the white, wrinkled flesh of his fingers. It was like clutching maggots. The U-boat captain grabbed hold of her face, and suddenly she couldn't breathe. There was a pressure in her ears as if she was under water. She tasted the burn of saltwater in her throat. Her vision speckled with black.

And suddenly she was knocked aside by a huge rush of water. Choking for breath, she was slammed into the wall as it sluiced past. Blearily she saw a shape being swept away by the water, kicking and screaming. Vida, helpless as a child caught in a flood.

She vanished from view around the corner. Rose got up again and gave chase. She saw that the corridor was already bone dry. Mickey was still slumped against the wall, rubbing his head in a daze, but Keisha was on her knees, slack-jawed, staring after the bizarre kidnappers.

'Look after Mickey,' she snapped. 'And tell the Doctor!'

'Don't leave me, Rose,' Keisha stammered. 'They could come back. What will I do if they come back?'

'Why ask me? You just proved I don't know a damn thing.'

'But Rose –'

'We ain't got time for this,' she snapped, pelting after Vida. 'Sort your life out, Keisha. No one's gonna do it for you.'

'Rose, you can't go chasing that stuff!'

I'm not just giving chase, she thought guiltily. *I'm running away.*

TWELVE

Even in the midst of her terror, Vida wondered if she was going barking mad. She was being washed out of her own offices, towed along like driftwood in the rapids. It was just too surreal.

The main door had been left open. *The steps*, she thought in a panic, *I'll break my back*. But the water seemed to solidify beneath her, made a kind of cushion as she slipped down on to the pavement.

She screamed, kicked and smashed at the water, but on it flowed down the street, carrying her away. *Will it stop at the traffic lights?* she wondered distantly, trying to impose some kind of logic on her situation. Then she saw the gaping hole ahead. A manhole cover stood propped against a parked car.

Oh, please, this isn't happening.

Helplessly, Vida plunged down into the blackness of the sewer. She heard the splash but felt nothing. She knew the sewers carried rainwater as well as waste in a combined system. And where did these overflow channels lead?

Where else? Out into the Thames…

The water coiled round her like a cold cocoon, protecting her as it rushed her away. *Is this what happened to you, Andrew?* Her mind fixed on the thought in the inky darkness. She was picking up speed, and tears began to ball in her throat. *Maybe I'll see you soon.*

Rose ran out into the middle of the road and stared all around. 'Vida?' she yelled. But the road was deserted: no trails, no signs of life at all. The street was quiet and empty.

The distant sirens sounded louder out here. They made a good soundtrack for her emotions. Where the hell had Vida gone? How could she just vanish? Rose started running again, in case she could maybe catch her up. It might have been a lost cause, but if truth were told she couldn't face Keisha and Mickey right now. Didn't even want to think about that. Swanning about on alien planets, she felt she had outgrown her former life; and yet this spiteful little home truth had grabbed her by the scruff of the neck and dumped her right back into the old days.

How *could* they…?

She shook her head, kept on running, pushed herself harder. Vida needed help and fast. If the water aliens had meant to kill her, they could have got her back in the building. So they must need her alive for some reason. But why?

Whatever, five got you ten they would be taking her back to Stanchion House. And what could *she* do about it?

The blare of sirens was getting louder. As she neared the bottom of the road, an ambulance and a large police van screeched from out of a side street. It stood to reason they were heading for the river. And since she was too…

The vehicles slowed down at the red traffic lights, checking the roads were clear before speeding on their way. Rose seized the moment and ran up behind the police van. Steeling herself, she jumped up lightly on to the back bumper and gripped hold of one of the handles in the blank double doors.

'Great, great plan, Rose,' she muttered. But this was a matter of life and death. With luck they would stop just round the corner, at the sight of a blonde woman being carted down the street by a runaway puddle.

'Hang in there, girl,' she murmured, both to Vida and to herself. Then, clinging on for dear life, she found herself hitching a ride riverwards.

The Doctor struggled up from the lab floor, but it felt more like he was pushing himself up from some dark, distant sea bed. He wasn't having this. 'I'm… not… like… humans,' he spat, pushing out the words with the last of his breath. 'You… can't… have… *me*.'

The water began to lose its strong taste. His mind began to clear. He clamped his eyes shut, felt water squeeze out, nodded furiously, willing himself on. 'Get out of me,' he shouted, and at last he could breathe again. 'Out!' he roared.

His face and clothes were dry, as if the attack had never happened. He rushed to the sink, but that was dry too. 'Where are you?' he yelled, turning on the taps. The water came out under enormous pressure, splashed out of the sink, soaked him properly this time, all over his waist and trousers.

'Doctor!'

'Mickey?' The Doctor spun about to face him, glanced down. 'OK, big wet patch on the trousers there. Looks dodgy, I know, but it's not what you think.'

'We were attacked,' Mickey panted. 'These jokers in fancy dress, they came out of the water.'

'They did? Oh. Yeah. I'll bet they did.' The Doctor ran over to check on him. 'Killing several birds with one wet stone. Reabsorb the water sample, try to suss me out since I'm not a local, and –'

'They've taken Vida,' said Mickey. 'Just sloshed her away in a load of water, right out of the door.'

'Rose went after her,' Keisha added, cowering back out in the corridor.

'Did she?' The Doctor winced. 'That wasn't very wise. Brave and adorable, yes, but not wise.'

Mickey shot a look at Keisha. 'Can't say I blame her for not hanging round.'

'You just did,' the Doctor said vaguely. 'Come on, think. Why would they take Vida?'

'How are we supposed to know what a puddle wants to do with its life?' Then Mickey froze. 'Hang on. This vice admiral bloke she was supposed to meet, 'cause her boss has gone missing. If she *can't* meet him, she can't blab, can she – and Crayshaw gets off the hook.'

'I don't think Crayshaw is too worried about some bigwig rapping his knuckles. But bigwigs do have their uses…'

'God, we were gonna tell you,' said Mickey. 'Crayshaw's old – we're talking 250 years old. He's in the naval records, same bloke. Drowned at sea.'

'The aliens got him,' said Keisha fearfully. 'But how can he be so ancient?'

The Doctor didn't look surprised in the slightest. 'The human body is 70 per cent water, and salt's a natural preservative. Throw in some alien biochemistry…'

'He was wearing shades when we saw him,' Mickey confirmed. 'He must have pearls for eyes, like the ones who whacked me. He's one of them.'

'Let's get to the Mickeymobile,' the Doctor said. 'We need to go to Stanchion House. These things will have taken Vida there.'

'You don't know that.'

'I bet you anything they have! How much do you wanna bet? Anything! Ten, twenty, fifty… a quid?'

Mickey shook his head wearily. 'So, what're we gonna do?'

'Break in, of course!'

'But there'll be soldiers everywhere!'

'I want to go back home,' said Keisha quietly. 'I can't deal with this. Please take me back so I can wait for my mum.'

Mickey glared at her. 'First we need to find Rose.'

'Shouldn't take long,' said the Doctor brightly. 'We'll grab her on the way. She can't have got far!'

'Omigod, omigod, omigod.' Rose was still clinging on to the back of the police van. She kept wanting to bang on the doors to make it stop, but didn't dare let go of the handles.

This had to rank as one of the dumbest things she'd ever done. Her heart was throbbing faster than the engine; the ground was blurring by – they had to be doing forty or fifty miles per hour around these streets. There was no sign of Vida anywhere and she had no feeling left in her fingers. Every time they took a corner her arms burned with the effort of keeping her balance.

But finally the van screeched to a halt near the river. Rose unhooked her fingers, tumbling to the ground with all the grace of a cartoon character who's just run into a brick wall. Aching everywhere, she scrambled underneath the vehicle, just as the back doors were flung open and the boys and girls in blue piled out.

'The driver was mad,' said someone, a few feet away.

'Tell me about it,' Rose muttered. She peered out from beneath the van and saw a police officer being comforted by a female colleague.

'Had to get to her sister, she said. Nothing else mattered.' He shook his head. 'She ran the blockade and then…'

Rose pulled herself from under the van and hurried for the cover of a nearby ambulance. But halfway across she got what they were talking about, and a sick feeling gripped her stomach.

The tail end of a double-decker bus was sticking out from the Thames's dark waters. Little police boats circled it like sharks. A huge hole gaped in the wall beside the river where it had ploughed through.

'What's happening?' the policeman went on. 'As fast as we block their way to the river, they break through.'

The woman squeezed his shoulder. 'Leave it to the soldier-boys. If they're so keen to deal with it, let them.'

Yeah, that's the spirit, thought Rose darkly, flitting between the parked vehicles, her way lit by blue flashes from their siren lights. She had to reach the river's edge without being seen – easier said than done, given the number of coppers and squaddies roaming about, arguing over who did what. Then her spirits rose a little as she recognised one of the boats moored to the wharf. Or rather the big tool kit and blanket on its deck, which were clearly PC Fraser's. Better still, there was no sign of anyone about. If he could only help her find Vida before it was too late…

She hurried down the steps to the small jetty. It was darker down here. The moon was just a faint circle half-buried by dark clouds.

By its feeble light, Rose saw the twitching bodies of a pair of soldiers on the jetty, clutching at their throats, mouthing in silent gasps.

So much for no one about.

She felt the hairs standing up on the back of her neck, turned to the boat. 'PC Fraser?' she called. 'You there?'

A dark shape appeared from inside the cabin, crossed the deck.

'Hello?' Rose said uncertainly. 'Fraser, you've seen someone, haven't you?'

'My mate, Fisky.' It was Fraser all right. She couldn't see him, but his voice sounded hoarse and strained. 'He couldn't tell me where the bodies were, 'cause he'd gone to join them.'

She walked steadily towards him. 'Let's talk about this, yeah?'

'He was my mate.' He turned, ducked out of sight. 'I've got to help him.'

The sound of the hefty splash tore through Rose like an explosion. 'No!' she shouted, as she bundled on to the boat. 'Whatever you saw, it wasn't him!'

She peered over the rail. Where was he? It was so dark, surely he couldn't have gone under already…

Then a blinding light bleached out the scene, as powerful floodlights were trained on the sunken bus from the river's edge. She flinched, lost her balance. Plunged head-first into the freezing river.

She turned a somersault in the water, kicked up with both legs to break the surface. Gasping and choking, she pushed her hair from her eyes, tried to blink away the water. *This is the Thames. What the hell am I gonna catch from being in here?*

Or what's gonna catch me?

Even as the grisly thought occurred to her, she felt something tug at her trainer. It pulled her down beneath the surface before she could draw breath. She kicked out, tried to free herself, but it was no good, she was being dragged down. Something bumped into her back – Fraser? Yeah, it must be Fraser coming to help her – he was a policeman after all, he would have heard her shouting to him…

Something sharp punctured the back of her neck.

Rose flailed furiously in the freezing water. But her lungs were already bursting, and a blood-red light was pressing in on her vision. At first she thought it was in her head. Then she realised a shifting landscape was resolving itself from the gloom, that vague and horrible shadows were drifting at a distance, all around her.

Terrified, she fought harder, and finally she kicked free of whatever it was dragging her under. Her clothes were weighing her down but she swam upwards, ignoring the steady throbbing at the base of her skull. She thought of nothing but propelling herself upwards, away from the red light, away from the *things*. She had no breath left, every movement hurt and dizzied her, but somehow she kept going.

She *had* to get away…

For Mickey, the night did not improve.

He drove the Doctor and Keisha around for hours but there was no sign of Rose or Vida anywhere. And all the roads down near the river were blocked off with barricades and soldiers, so they couldn't even get to the most likely places. He drove past a hospital in Westminster and wondered if he should go in and ask about new arrivals. But stuff was clearly kicking off there. People were swarming round the entrance like flies round rotten fruit. The Doctor wasted no time poking his nose in and found that the number of dehydrated people was on the increase – but no sign of Rose and Vida.

'Our ghosts are keeping busy. But what do they want, besides a quick glug?' He turned to Keisha. 'You haven't seen Jay again?'

'No,' she said, and sounded so sad about it. She kept quiet for the rest of the ride. Shame she couldn't have watched her mouth when it really mattered.

Don't go over that again, Mickey told himself.

There was a definite uneasy atmosphere brewing in the city, he could feel it. The endless sirens, people spilling in and out of hospitals, wanting answers, getting nothing. And blocking off the river only fed the rumours of disappearing people. The sight of so many soldiers on the streets didn't help matters – it implied the police couldn't cope, that some sort of national emergency was in progress. But listening to the news there was no statement, no announcement. No one knew what the emergency actually *was*, just that it was going on around them.

Now here they were back on the estate, with the dawn breaking. Mickey kept wishing and wishing in his head that they would find Rose safe and sound at Jackie's place. They had to find her, and she *had* to be OK. The thought that something bad had happened to her straight after hearing about *that* night – the night he couldn't even remember…

Mickey walked Keisha up the stairs to her flat in silence, while the Doctor waited for them in the car. Keisha fumbled for her keys.

'I didn't know this was gonna happen,' she said, pushing open the door. 'How *could* I have known?'

Mickey shrugged. 'Just find whatever stuff you need, and start writing your note. I wanna get off to Jackie's.'

She nodded. 'I need to find her too, Mickey. I've gotta talk to her.'

'Ain't you said enough?'

'I've got to. 'Cause…' Keisha took a deep breath. ''Cause… it never happened.'

He frowned. 'What?'

'Us. That night.' She didn't look at him. 'It was me who tried it on, not you. But you didn't want to know. You crashed out, and I let you think we'd…'

'You made it up?' Mickey stared at her, conflicted, wanting to believe her but not daring to let himself off the hook. 'Serious?'

'I ain't used to it, Mickey. Rejection, I mean. Getting boys is the one thing I *can* do.'

'But Rose is your mate. One of your best mates.'

'I know. I ain't proud of what I –'

'Which is why you put the blame on me,' he realised.

'I know you never liked me. That's sort of why I wanted you.' She snorted. 'I know it was stupid, but you kept going on about how she'd pushed off and left us all, how she didn't care and was never coming back, and that hurt me, Mickey, just like it hurt you. That she could just go off like that.'

He shook his head, incredulous. 'And what, you wanted to get back at her by copping off with me?'

She looked at him at last. 'I dunno what I wanted.'

'But you knew it made you feel like dirt,' said Mickey. 'Which is why you had to punish *me* for what never happened.' He could feel his anger building. 'The bricks through the window, the stories you spread, the blokes you got to rough me up – all 'cause of *nothing*?'

Keisha walked over to the cluttered dining table, started writing her note on the back of an envelope.

'So how come you told Rose that rubbish?'

She kept on writing.

'*How come?*'

''Cause I ain't forgiven her, Mickey,' she snapped, slamming down the pen. 'She's my mate and I love her, but she's changed. She's like a different person now she's with that Doctor.'

'And you wonder why you drive people away!'

'You can see she's changed. You *know* it.'

'Maybe I do,' he said. 'But I still love her, whoever she is.' He slumped down on her sofa. 'Now go on, finish your note,' he said more quietly. 'Go pack whatever stuff you need. Then we're out of here.' He should have felt elated, he supposed, or mad with anger. But he just felt tired. Tired and scared, because that nagging voice that kept telling him he would never see Rose again was growing louder and louder.

He jumped as the tinny little tune of a mobile phone broke the heavy silence. 'That ain't yours, is it?'

'Like it would be,' she said. 'Oh, God. It must be that old woman's.'

'Her name was Anne,' said Mickey, and picked up the chunky handset. 'Do I answer?'

'I dunno.'

He bottled it, and let the phone ring on. But as the tune stopped dead, he noticed the display: 23 MISSED CALLS.

'Someone's off their head with worry,' he murmured. She had a stack of voicemails waiting, and he found himself dialling the answerphone number as prompted.

'You have fourteen new messages. First message:…'

A woman's voice spoke softly in his ear. 'Anne? It's your sister, I've just seen you but… Oh, Anne, it can't be you, can it? You can't be under the Thames.'

Mickey felt the mother of all chills mess with his spine, put the mobile on speakerphone.

'It's a trick, it must be,' Anne's sister went on, halting, clearly trying not to cry. 'Tell me it's a trick, Anne. When you get this, tell me you're OK.' She paused, then rang off.

'Anne's one of them too.' He looked at Keisha. 'She's turned into a ghost-thing like Jay.'

'She can't have,' said Keisha. 'She was never on the *Ascendant*. How –'

A man's voice came on the line next, reedy, agitated: 'Anne, it's David. The weirdest thing just happened, I saw you – thought I saw you, anyway, in my front room – and you told me you… Well, it's stupid, I know, but it was so real. I can't get hold of you at home. *Please*, when you get this, call and let me know you're OK.' A pause. 'See, this image I saw, it said something about the drowned, and I know you're still raw from poor Peter going –'

Mickey killed the call. 'The same thing's happening. They drown, they come back, they trick *more* people into drowning. First the ship's crew, haunting the people they love. Then those people haunt the people *they* love. Sort of like a cycle – don't you get it? That's why London's so mad tonight – the effect's spreading. It's gonna *keep* spreading!' He stood up. 'Come on, we've got to tell the Doctor, let him hear this.'

But Keisha was staring past him, at the doorway. She was trembling.

He turned. It felt as if he was moving in slow motion.

Rose was standing there. Large as life, picked out in pale colour. She looked scared half to death and dripping wet.

'Oh, Mickey, Keish, you've got to help me,' she said, her lips out of synch with the words. 'Say you'll help me.' She gave them an encouraging smile and a trickle of water ran from her nose. 'Help me before the feast.'

THIRTEEN

The water washed away from Vida and her senses began to return. She was in a dank, dark hole. The ground was wet and hard, rocking gently beneath her. The ceiling rustled above her; it was a piece of thick canvas, stirred by the wind. A rasping, shushing sound, like pipes gurgling, added an eerie soundtrack.

Other things were stirring around her in the darkness. She could hear slithers, dragging sounds, but the weird acoustics offered no clue as to where they were actually coming from.

'Who's there?' she whispered, trying to stop herself shivering.

'You are unharmed?'

She started. That sounded like Crayshaw's voice. 'Where the hell am I?'

'I believe this was once the *Ascendant*'s storeroom. You are in a part of the aft section, towed here by the tug.' He chuckled softly. 'Crayshaw would think of it as a Trojan Horse. He had an appreciation of the classics.'

'You creatures were hiding inside the *Ascendant*,' she

realised. 'Used it to get yourselves brought here.'

'Humans enjoy puzzles. They have such inquiring little minds.'

'What are you? Where are you from?'

'Ah, the names. How you love to know names and dates and places, to pin down facts and arrange them in neat order.' Crayshaw paused. 'We have no name. Our history is irrelevant. We live, and we spread. We are of the waterhive.'

'So you dismantled the *Ascendant* under water just to intrigue us?' She nodded, reasoning it out. 'And I suppose Commodore Powers told you it was coming your way – he's your advance scout, right? Thrown back from the sea to prepare the way for you. Ensuring that the pieces of the ship would be taken straight here to a key naval establishment, a secret stronghold. And then you could use that secrecy against us.'

A deeper chill sounded in his voice. 'Your intelligence is sound, Miss Swann.'

'Unlike your body, I'll bet. After 250 years it must be wearing a bit thin.' No reply. She went on, trying to keep her voice steady, 'I suppose Powers fixed you up with a fake personnel file, as well as helping to put you in charge of this mess.'

'It is a pity you were not killed when you tried to leave this place with the Doctor,' said Crayshaw.

She heard more scuffling in the dark, wondered if this thing could see how scared she must look. 'Are you after the filament tracers on board the *Ascendant*?' He didn't answer her. 'Have they been poisoning your sea water? Or do you plan to use them against us somehow?'

'We can manipulate all moisture as we choose. Your technology means nothing to us.'

'Without it we would never have learned you were here,' she realised. 'No wonder you wanted me out of the way.'

'We suspected your department knew something of our activities,' Crayshaw agreed. 'But Andrew Dolan knows so very little, while you know a great deal.'

She shut her eyes, though it made no difference to the blackness. 'You took him when you saw him.'

'And drowned him.' A soft chuckle. 'He is ours, now. He was to have dealt with Vice Admiral Kelper on our behalf. Now he is being put to a different use, and you will meet Kelper in his place.'

'What have you done to Andrew?' she hissed.

As she spoke, a ghostly light stole into the room. The stooped, brittle form of Crayshaw was revealed, standing just in front of her. And now, swelling from the centre of the supernatural light, she could see Andrew, his full, proud features just as dear and familiar as if he was sitting in his office chair. But he was so pale, and when he spoke the image seemed to ripple like a puddle at the end of a rainstorm.

'Help me, Vida,' he breathed. 'Save me, before the feast.'

'You're not real,' she whispered, fear clawing at her guts.

'Only you can save me. You must come to me.'

'No!' she shouted.

He looked stung, affronted. Then he smiled. Water gushed from his nose and eyes as he seemed to glow brighter.

And now Vida could see what else was with her in the

shadowy belly of this piece of the ship. The gurgling sound wasn't pipes. It was people, rasping for breath, slashes in their cheeks and neck quivering like little mouths. She saw the real Andrew among them, shuffling on the spot, moaned in horror at the sight of the dark lines of blood trailing slowly down his face.

And there was Rose Tyler, her face just as ghoulish, staring sightlessly with shiny eyes.

'Are… are they dead?'

'Our creatures must acclimatise,' Crayshaw explained. 'They were herded here along the river bed. Soon they will learn to draw their oxygen exclusively from water. The gills we have grown for them will serve them well. Perhaps now you see why poor Mr Dolan cannot meet the vice admiral?'

It was sick, horrible. 'You can live on land easily enough, why can't he?'

'The trauma to his body is too fresh, his new anatomy not yet stable.' He gestured to himself. 'Total mastery of the human body and its appearance as you see here is only possible after years of cellular integration.'

'Why are you doing this?' she hissed. 'And why is Kelper so important to you?'

'For the same reasons he is important to you, my dear,' said Crayshaw blandly. 'His authority, his office, the fleets he commands. These are necessary to us.'

'Don't you think the naval brass might notice he's grown gills and pearly eyes? You just said it took years to look even as normal as you do!'

'His voice on the phone. His codes on a computer. These

are all we require.' He nodded. 'And you will help us to procure them.'

'Only if you make Andrew better,' she said. 'Him and all these people. Make them normal again.'

'Oh, we could do that,' Crayshaw agreed, 'as easily as doing nothing at all.'

'Turn them back and I... I promise I'll help you.'

'Very well.'

Vida felt a tiny surge of hope. But as the ghost of Andrew dribbled away to nothing and his light faded, she caught the supercilious smile on Crayshaw's face and knew the thing was lying. She was back in darkness, the wheezing, rasping breath of the drowned still dragging in her ears.

'The vice admiral will be landing soon. You will contact him and arrange your meeting at a place of our choosing.'

'Who *are* you?' she screamed.

'We are of the waterhive.' The voice was different. It was softer, spookier, almost feminine, though it came from where Crayshaw was standing. 'And the hour of the feast is fast approaching.'

A new noise started up. A slithering, slapping noise, like a fish writhing on dry ground in the throes of dying. Only this sounded more like excitement, a sort of horrible applause all around her. These alien creatures of the deep were still hidden here in the cracks and crannies of the hulk, waiting, anticipating.

And with a sick feeling she knew that whatever she did, they would use her to help them make their plans a reality.

* * *

'Yes, I saw Rose too,' was all the Doctor would say. He strode through the walkways of the estate with a look in his dark eyes that said *do not mess*. Mickey could hardly keep up with him.

'We've got to go to her,' said Keisha.

'She's right. Rose needs us,' said Mickey. 'Now. We can't muck about.'

The Doctor didn't break his step, didn't turn. 'Shut up,' he said.

'But she's in danger, like Jay!' Keisha insisted. 'We have to get to her before the feast –'

'Shut up, shut up, shut up!' The Doctor whirled on one heel and rounded on them both. 'This whole planet could be in danger! D'you think I don't want to go jumping into the Thames after Rose? You think I don't want to…' He pinched the bridge of his nose, closed his eyes, trying to get a hold of himself. 'I *do* want to, and I didn't even see her clearly. My senses are about a thousand times smarter than yours. These creatures haven't got the measure of me yet, haven't learned how to press all my buttons. But they're having a damned good go.' His eyes snapped open, urgent and soulful. 'Now listen to me, both of you. You know that those critters in the river are fishing for humans, and they're not throwing them back. Knowing that is making it easier for your brains to fight against the alien effect, so keep reminding yourself of what you saw back at Vida's offices. Don't trust the voices in your head, don't trust these images of Rose – trust *me*.'

Mickey considered. 'What're you gonna do?'

'First of all, you're both going to help me fight a dragon.'

Keisha grimaced. 'Dragon?'

'You! How *dare* you show your face round here!'

The Doctor pointed upwards to where Rose's mum, Jackie, was hanging over the edge of the balcony, deafening the dawn like hell in a fluffy pink nightie. Her hair was a rat's maze, her face red and tear-streaked.

'Happy now, are you? Now you finally got her killed?' She hurled a carton of milk down at him, which missed by a mile and burst open on the concrete. 'My Rose is a ghost! We've got to save her!'

'Rose isn't a ghost. Promise,' the Doctor called back up, reasonably. 'You're being tricked!'

'By aliens, I suppose?'

'Well, actually…'

'I don't want your excuses!'

'Look, I'll just pop up, shall I?'

Mickey could see curtains twitching as he followed the Doctor up the steps. Someone yelled incoherent abuse at all the shouting. And in the distance, still the sirens called mournfully to each other. *How long before everyone here's got someone in the river?* he thought. *Or else someone dried up in intensive care.'*

'Look,' said Keisha. A milkman was sprawled at the top of the stairwell. 'I guess… the Rose ghost did that when it came to see Jackie. Right?'

'Right. Well done.' The Doctor picked the man up. 'Luckily he doesn't look too bad. Probably other cases in the nearby flats. As the ghosts grow in number, they'll take less water from more victims.'

Mickey hazarded a guess as to why. 'Because they want their victims able to chuck themselves in the Thames?'

'Very good, Mickey. There is a brain in there!'

'You're gonna get yours battered when Jackie arrives.' Mickey could hear her thundering along the concrete balcony towards the steps. 'What're you gonna do with the milkman, use him as a human shield?'

'Peace offering. Jackie's not a bad nurse, and right now I'd say she needs someone to look after.' The Doctor propped up the milkman against Keisha and gave her a sharp look. 'You must stay with Jackie, right? Look after her, help her with this fella and do *not* let her out the house. Whatever she says, whatever Jay says –'

'OK,' she blurted. 'I'll try.'

'And what about me?' said Mickey. 'Surplus to requirements again?'

'Don't be silly, you're full of good ideas,' the Doctor chided. Then, as Jackie loomed up, he stepped nimbly behind him. 'Human shield.'

Jackie glowered at the Doctor. 'I don't know how you can live with yourself.'

'I'm going to get Rose back,' he said.

'But she's dying, *drowning*!'

'Yes!' the Doctor cried, shoving Mickey aside like some random obstacle crowding his genius. 'The dead are no good to these aliens. But they can merge with humans as they drown, use anti-cellularisation to rework the body… So that at the point of human death, something altogether more malleable is born.'

'Don't try and trick me with your clever talk,' stormed Jackie. 'I *saw* her!'

'It's the chemistry that's clever here, not the chat.' The Doctor went to her solemnly, took hold of her hands. Mickey held his breath. 'I won't lie to you. Rose is in great danger. She's been got by the enemy, whoever they are. And like Jay, like all the others, she's needed to lure people like you into the water, so you can go on to lure all the people *you* love…' He broke off, glanced back at Mickey and winced. 'Blimey, that's gonna be a *right* motley assortment!'

Jackie's face clouded. Mickey winced as she whacked the Doctor hard round the face.

'Ow!' he gasped, staggered back. 'Was I being rude? OK, guessing that *was* rude.'

For a moment, Mickey thought Jackie was about to go for the Doctor again. But the rage had left her, and big tears were welling up in her eyes. She turned to Keisha and burst into noisy sobs, tried to hug her but ended up with a fair bit of milkman in her grip.

The Doctor rubbed his red cheek. 'OK. Mix a teaspoon of salt, one of baking powder, four tablespoons of sugar, a cup of orange juice and a pint of water, and get it down Milko's neck,' he told Keisha, turning to leave. 'Lots of little sips.'

'Where are you going?' she asked, stroking Jackie's shuddering back.

'London's going down the tubes.' He looked mournful, still rubbing his cheek. 'And I suppose I am too.'

'What does that mean?' Mickey frowned. 'What are you going to do?'

But the Doctor simply jogged back down the steps. Mickey went after him, worried by the silence. Either the Doctor was playing the moody alien whose ideas were too big for mere mortal brains to grasp, or else he didn't have a clue.

Not that, thought Mickey, the angry swoop of circling choppers overhead vying with the drone of sirens. *Don't let it be that.*

FOURTEEN

As if she was in some horrible dream, Rose found herself taking slow-mo steps through the inky water. There was a pressure in her head, and beneath that a sort of prickling, tickling, stinging feeling. Like little insects with blowtorches were welding odd bits of her brain together.

She tried to ignore it, to concentrate on breathing. Her chest no longer rose and fell; it felt numb, dead flesh. She was aware only of a burning itch on both cheeks as she walked one step after the other, sliding through the thick Thames mud, tripping over slimy obstacles. She saw everything around her in a sick green light, half-lurching, half-swimming onwards with the others until they reached the narrow mouth of a pipe in the dark wall.

Two creatures that might once have been men guarded it. They looked like pale, translucent corpses. Their eyes were like big grey jellyfish eating into their faces.

'Go through,' one croaked, standing aside. Rose heard him clear as day – how could that be when she was under water? She pondered the riddle as she squeezed after the others into the pipeline, dragged herself along through the water. Someone crawled in front of her, someone behind. She didn't know who they were. But it didn't matter.

They were all a part of the hive now.

Not for the first time, Mickey was wondering how come he ever let the Doctor talk him into doing anything.

He'd meant it about going down the tubes. Or more accurately, down Aldgate tube. It was now 6 a.m. and the underground station was just opening.

Mickey eyed the ticket barrier. 'Gonna use your sonic screwdriver?'

The Doctor seemed affronted. 'Do I look like your average fare dodger?'

'Yeah. A bit.'

'Cheeky. Get yourself a single. And get me one too, while you're at it.'

Once through the barriers, the Doctor ran down to the empty platform and sonicked open a STAFF ONLY door in the side of the wall. It gave on to a little cupboard space full of hard hats, torches, emergency equipment. Leading off from there was a narrow access corridor, ending in another locked door, marked for authorised service personnel only. Soon the hum of the screwdriver was filling the little room.

'You any good with phones?' he asked.

'Only at running up bills,' Mickey said.

With the lock shocked to bits, the Doctor opened the door to reveal a cramped, circular tunnel, sloping downwards at an alarming angle. The walls were a thick spaghetti of coloured wiring all the way round. Thick plastic bands grouped the wires into bunches and provided footholds.

'Phone lines. Secret government link-up, in case of nuclear war,' the Doctor whispered. 'This is hidden London, Mickey.'

'It can stay hidden,' he replied, turning up his nose. 'It's horrible. Look at those webs. No one's been down here for years.'

'Till now. Because what Crayshaw and his mates don't seem to realise is that this conduit passes within just a few inches of the decontamination chamber. And from there we can get inside and face these creatures in their lair.' He grinned. 'I know where that is, by the way. Passed it while I was on the run from the marines – never even knew! That's the thing about hindsight, it's always twenty-twenty.'

'So you can get us inside – maybe. What then?'

'I need to talk with these creatures.'

'They didn't seem keen on talking when they called by before, did they?' Mickey protested. 'What d'you think they're gonna do – put the kettle on and give you a biscuit?'

'Wouldn't that be marvellously civilised!' His grin faded. 'If I'm going to stop them, I need to know what it is I'm going to stop. Cheer up – now their evil plans are in full swing and nothing stands in their way, maybe they'll be feeling chattier.'

'Yeah. Cheerful thought.' He frowned, pointed to the tunnel. 'Hang on, you said this goes past a few inches from that chamber thing, right? A few inches of what?'

'Solid concrete.'

'You are so joking me!'

'It's all right!' The Doctor brandished the sonic screwdriver.

'I'm getting quite good at resonating concrete.'

'Well, *I'm* getting freaked at the thought of going down there.'

'It's probably the best place we could be,' the Doctor told him. 'Not many people about to filch water from. Less chance of Rose's image coming back to haunt us both.' He started to climb inside, then glanced back and fixed Mickey with his large, piercing eyes. 'I don't want to see her like that again. Do you?'

Mickey climbed in after him, and they began their cautious descent into the narrow passage.

Strung out with nerves, aching with tiredness, Vida wondered what time it was. Andrew, Rose, all those poor people had been pushed into the river, unprotesting, off like livestock to the slaughter. Soon, Crayshaw assured her, there would be more victims 'acclimatising' in the darkness.

To her uneasy relief she had been moved on to dry land. The morning sun was rising steadily, yet there was no one about on this side of the bank. Across the bridge it was a circus of police cars, troop carriers and ambulances as a yelling, jostling swarm of people pressed in on the roadblocks and barriers. It was pointless even to think of shouting for help, and clearly Crayshaw knew it. He had seized her arm in a punishing grip and marched her into the reception of Stanchion House.

Hope flickered as the glass doors slid open. If she could only signal to somebody that she was in trouble…

Not a chance. The place was entirely deserted. No

receptionist. No Derek guarding the lifts. Nobody.

'Where is everyone?' she demanded. 'What have you done with them?'

'Arrange the meeting with Kelper,' said Crayshaw.

'Why can't you do it yourself?'

'I am deemed to be obstructive. It will be easier if he suspects nothing. Call him on your personal phone.'

She pulled her mobile from her pocket. If only the water had damaged it, if only...

'I'm out of power,' she said, disbelievingly. 'The battery's dead. His private cell number's programmed in and I can't access it!' She thrust the phone in Crayshaw's old face, triumphantly. Whatever happened, at least she knew she couldn't be held accountable. She hadn't helped these things, and whatever they did now –

'Vida? What the hell is going on around here? I just strolled in. What the hell has happened to security?'

She jumped as if she'd been poked with a stick. A massive man in full naval dress uniform was striding towards them, brass, brocade and decorations shining in the strong reception lights. It was him, Kelper, accompanied by a young aide.

'All London's gone crazy.' The vice admiral's nasal tones filled the reception like the drone of an engine. 'I had to fly in to Bletchley and take a chopper out here. Couldn't reach Andrew, or you –'

Vida opened her mouth to speak, but Crayshaw got there first: 'We can reach Andrew.'

Her mouth dried. She offered a hopeless look of vague

apology, then watched Crayshaw with frightened eyes as the two men exchanged formal greetings.

'Miss Swann informs me you have arrived to inspect the wreck of the *Ascendant* yourself, Vice Admiral,' said Crayshaw.

Kelper spoke frankly. 'Your administration of this affair seems to be a mess, John. I've found government ministers chasing their tails, a lack of communication between the naval ranks, a general absence of explanation as to how the *Ascendant* came to be in bits at the bottom of the sea... A conspiracy of silence which extends to the fate and whereabouts of certain chemical tracers Miss Swann's department had placed upon that ship.'

'There is no conspiracy, I assure you,' said Crayshaw, all smiles, crossing to the lift. 'You must inspect our underground laboratories for yourself.'

The doors slid smoothly open.

'Must we go now?' said Vida awkwardly. 'Perhaps we should adjourn to one of the briefing rooms and –'

'The sooner this matter is ended, the better,' he said casually. 'And Andrew Dolan is already down there. We should really see how he is faring.'

Kelper and his aide looked inquiringly at Vida. She looked at the floor, her frantic thoughts piling up, crowding her head. This thing held Andrew, Rose, so many others in its power, and if she messed up now they would never be saved. But then, was there even the tiniest chance that this hive thing wearing Crayshaw's body would keep its word, whatever she did?

'Run!' she shouted suddenly, grabbing hold of Kelper's

braided sleeve, and yanking him away from Crayshaw. He hesitated, confused. She tugged on his arm again, dragged him away. 'He needs something from you, I don't know what!'

The aide seemed about to protest when Crayshaw grabbed him by the back of the neck and flung him with superhuman force inside the lift. He smashed head-first against the wall and slumped down.

'How many more times!' Vida yelled. '*Run!*'

She started to drag Kelper after her. But as she heard water splash under her soles, she knew it was already too late.

A carnival procession of pale, bloated freaks stood blocking the turnstiles out of the reception. Her blood chilled at the sight of the Victorian lady, the pirate and the U-boat captain who had come for her before, their eyes silvery, fat and ruined. But there were many others now: a dark-haired child in Regency lace, a group of young sailors in bell-bottoms, an old man in a stained apron. They stood ranged in silence, water trickling steadily from their noses and mouths.

'As I said, sir…' Crayshaw had removed his dark glasses, and now they could see the scabrous pearls that bulged obscenely from under his lids. 'The sooner this matter is ended, the better.'

Rose felt the bodies crushing in around her. How many were there now in the black reaches of this flooded pit? She shut out the thought. It was easier, better to think of the faces in her head. A blonde woman, care and concern behind the glare in her eyes, her scent so familiar and warm Rose could cry. *Mum? Mum, where are you?* A man, burly and staring with close-cropped hair – no, that image blurred into another, youthful and friendly with quirky good looks. His eyes gleamed with secrets he would share only with her, and... *Doctor, I want you here...* a black boy with a scally smile and warm arms... *Mickey, say you never did that...* girl-friends reeking of clubs and smoke and hastily sucked mints... *I trusted you...*

They would come to her. Yes, that was a lovely thought. They cared and they would come to get her out of here before the feast began.

Keisha was drifting in and out of an uneasy sleep, totally drained. Her life felt so messed up and mixed around she had become numb to it. Now and then, something would jolt her awake – the sound of Jackie fussing over the parched stranger in her bed, or the grave voice of the man on the TV news.

'...putting guards on the sewers to stop them getting into the Thames that way. The number of people drawn to the river from all over the country continues to grow, and the terrifying possibility remains that soon the army will be unable to hold them back...'

Keisha hit the mute button, a low, panicky feeling in her stomach. Her mum should have called by now. Had she not got the note asking her to call? What if she'd not called in, and had gone straight to the river instead? The thought gnawed at her.

Soon she pulled out her mobile and dialled the mobile number she'd 1471ed back at the flat. The number her mum had called on.

Just the answerphone. She hung up. Her mum sounded happy, perky on the message. She'd never sounded that way when she'd been home.

'It's all going to pot,' said Jackie softly, joining Keisha on the sofa. 'Everyone's going out of their minds.'

Keisha put away the phone. 'They're being tricked.'

'And there's not even any spaceships in the sky.'

'We've gotta stay right here,' Keisha told her, and Jackie nodded. 'Whatever happens, we know it ain't real.' She paused. 'I hope my mum gets here soon.'

'I wish *my* mum was here,' Jackie agreed, feeling for Keisha's hand. She found it – then squeezed hard, hard enough to break fingers. There was a strangled gasp from the bedroom, as if the milkman could feel the pain too.

'Ow! Jackie, what're you –'

Then Keisha saw the ghost of Rose, sad-eyed and dripping, in front of the TV. The image stared at them, saying nothing.

'Mickey never did nothing,' said Keisha, trembling. 'I made it up. I was stupid, I…'

But the ghost of Rose just opened up her arms, ready to give them both a big, wet hug. 'Please,' she whispered.

'I'm coming, sweetheart,' said Jackie, and Keisha was already getting up off the sofa, crossing to the door.

Rose looked so grateful as she splashed away to nothing.

'We've been crawling through these tunnels for ever,' Mickey complained, his voice sounding unnaturally loud in the confined space. 'When are we gonna get somewhere?'

'We *are* somewhere,' the Doctor retorted, ducking down a

new path in this cramped maze of concrete and spaghetti wiring. 'Junction X2, there you go, says so on the wall.'

'Junction X2? What's that supposed to mean?'

'Means we're probably close to the decon chamber.'

'Means we're lost!'

'We are not lost. I don't do lost.'

Mickey nodded to himself. 'We're lost.'

'Not listening.'

'Lost!'

'Blah, blah, blah, can't hear you.'

On they went through the concrete catacombs.

Vida was shoved into the lift after Kelper, propelled by cold, dead hands.

'What the hell is happening?' He stared in horror at the ice-white, bloated faces pressing in around them, crowding into the enclosed space, trampling the aide underfoot. 'What are these things?'

'Creatures from space,' Vida gasped as the lift door slid closed. 'The source of those alien proteins in the sea samples.'

'We are close to the spawning time,' said Crayshaw over the smooth whine of the lift descending. 'And so you are needed, Vice Admiral Kelper. The ships of your navy must help to spread us. We must create new power bases. Harbours. Inlets. Great lakes. All will be as one with us.'

Kelper sneered and shook his head. 'You're crazy.'

Crayshaw replaced his dark glasses. 'You will soon come to see things as we do.'

Vida looked over at Kelper, feeling sick with fear. 'He's

going to drown us.' Then the pirate's fingers wormed over her lips, rubbery and wet like tentacles, silencing her as the lift softly jarred to a stop. The Victorian woman did the same to Kelper as the doors whooshed open.

There was a clatter, a sudden hubbub, and at once Vida saw why the building above ground had seemed so deserted. Everyone was down here in the secret labs. Soldiers, security guards, cleaners, they milled about in this vast, antiseptic landscape of gleaming tiles and plastic partitions, dwarfed by the ship cross-sections that littered the space like unlikely sculptures.

The squad leader came forward to address Crayshaw while his fellows held back, staring uneasily as the sinister crowd spilled from the lift. 'Sir, we've been waiting for your orders. Surely the protection of this building and the wreck outside should be our priority, not these labs?'

'We've all been stuck down here for hours,' snapped the cleaning woman, clearly too tired and angry to be afraid, 'while you're mucking about having a fancy-dress party. I've got to get on, you know!'

Everyone jumped except Crayshaw as the doors to the decontamination room ground open. Heads craned to watch the dark hole open up like a wound in the sterile chamber. Vida tensed herself but nothing and nobody came out. She struggled in the icy grip of the pirate ghoul, tried to speak through his thick, wrinkled fingers, but it was no good.

'Sir?' The squad leader turned back to Crayshaw, edgy and uncertain. 'Your orders, sir?'

Suddenly, with a rushing, thundering roar, a wave of filthy

water came flooding in through the decon doors. It smashed against the remnants of the *Ascendant* with incredible force, as if eager to pound them to nothing. And as it sped towards the horrified crowd it seemed to rear up like some impossible animal. Guns exploded in a deafening rattle as the soldiers fired wildly, uselessly into the grey, churning mass.

'Your orders are to drown for us, soldier,' called Crayshaw. 'We no longer require your protection. But don't fear. As the spark of life leaves your bodies, newness will awaken inside you.'

Vida and the vice admiral were thrust forward to join the others. The body of the aide was thrown after them, knocking Vida to the gleaming floor. And as the water crashed down towards her, she saw Crayshaw had cracked a happy grin.

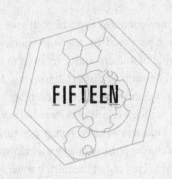

FIFTEEN

Vida shut her eyes as the water came gushing and seething onwards. Then the wall above the decontamination chamber exploded.

A welter of concrete boulders, tiles and shrapnel boomed out in an awesome dust cloud, then splashed down into the torrent of water to create an impromptu dam. The filthy wave broke over her and the others but seemed somehow robbed of its force, as if the blow had somehow weakened it.

The echoes of the explosion and the impact spun round the enormous room with deafening force. Crayshaw gave an inhuman shriek of fury, but carrying above it came a very human-sounding voice.

'Ha! Now that's what I *call* resonating concrete!'

'Doctor!' Vida yelled.

He was crouched on one knee, that screwdriver thing of his clamped in one hand, laughing with the air of a man who couldn't quite believe what he'd done. Well, neither could anybody else, but what did that matter? She was already up and running towards him.

'Come on!' she shouted to the others. 'It's the cavalry!'

The ones not paralysed by fear and shock – Kelper, the cleaner, a handful of soldiers – ran after her. But Crayshaw and his barmy buddies weren't distracted for long. The water was soon seething around their feet, thickening like wallpaper paste, sucking at their heels. *We can control all moisture…*

'Come on!' That was Mickey, trying not to choke on the dust. 'You can climb up the rubble, we'll help you!'

Vida dragged herself out of the miring water, scrambled up the rock pile, scratching her hands, bruising her legs. The Doctor reached out to her, hauled her up the rest of the way. For a giddy moment she felt safe at last, as Mickey pulled her from the precipice and into a cramped circular passage wreathed with wiring.

Mickey looked accusingly at the Doctor. 'This don't look like a decontamination chamber to me.'

'I was close,' the Doctor said defensively. 'It's just down there! Wasn't I close, Vida?'

Vida hugged him. 'Close enough for me.'

Kelper pulled himself through the hole in the wall. 'I don't know what the hell's going on, nor who you are,' he spluttered, 'but those are *aliens*.'

'Oh, d'you think?' The Doctor affected puzzlement. Then he noticed a red-haired soldier struggling up the pile of concrete. 'Private Jodie North!' he shouted. She reached frantically for his outstretched hand and he hauled her up. 'I pinched your pass. Sorry, hope it didn't cause you too much bother.'

She looked down to find he'd somehow sneaked it into her palm. 'No thanks,' she said, thrusting it into Vida's hands instead. 'I'm going AWOL.' She nodded briefly before retreating into the cable-strewn tunnel.

'We're going to need Torchwood,' Kelper muttered.

'We're going to need all our wits and a lot of luck,' snapped the Doctor. 'And more people would be good. More recruits.' He peered out through the smashed concrete. 'Excuse me, your planet needs you. Any volunteers?'

'Oh, God.' Vida saw that the rest of the crowd were trapped in the water. It had frozen to ice around them. Only the cleaner stood a chance – she had managed to pull one foot clear and was working to free the other one.

The Doctor jumped down from his precarious ledge to help her. He grabbed a lump of concrete and hammered at the ice.

'Where'd all this water come from?' Mickey wondered.

'The Thames, I suppose,' said Vida. 'There's a way up from the drainage pit to the river. It's how…' She swallowed. 'People have been sent down there, through the water. That's how they flooded the drainage area in the first place – they must have just sloshed in more water. Like the burst tank back at the offices – they can *influence* water…'

'Yeah, I see that,' croaked Mickey.

Crayshaw was coming to get them. His gruesome army had burst apart like water balloons, one by one; now he rode the resultant stream of water in his shades like an aged surfer. Towards the Doctor.

Rose stirred as the currents in the water raced past her limbs. The slipstream actually tugged her up from her knees to her feet, and for a moment she felt the terrible cold of the water around her.

With the cold came an awful clarity. *I shouldn't be here.* She struck out through the darkness, pushed against the bodies all around her. *Keep calm.* If she could only find a way out...

Then a face shoved up against hers. The ponderous face of a middle-aged man.

'You're *thinking*,' he said fiercely. 'Hold on to those thoughts. New ideas. Fresh thinking, that's what's needed...'

'Who are you?' Rose said out loud. A few bubbles came from her mouth; it felt wrong, all wrong to be speaking under water and to hear the sounds as clear as you like. That set her more on edge, focussed her further. She could see the glint of her long blonde hair as it waved slowly all about her. 'What's happened?'

'My name's Huntley,' the man said. 'Your mind is being influenced, but you *can* fight it. Some people are trying, I help them as much as I can.'

'As much... as you can.' Rose was feeling drowsy again. The faces were starting to crowd back into her head.

'Stay with me, girl! What's your name?'

'Rose... I'm Rose.'

'Yes. Well, Rose, I'm a scientist, and let me tell you – ordinarily I would dismiss something as unlikely and ludicrous as our predicament here in a moment. Only the Doctor was right, d'you see –'

'Doctor?' She felt a jolt of energy shock her awake again, grabbed hold of his arm, looked into his pearly eyes. 'You know the Doctor?'

'He's not a GP, Rose.'

'You met him in the underground labs, yeah?'

Huntley's eyes glimmered as they widened. 'Yes.'

'The Doctor's my friend. He's… He's the only one who can help us, but I don't know where he is…' Rose's eyes felt sore and hot. 'I wish I did. I've been thinking about him –'

'And trying to bring him here to you.' Huntley nodded. 'You must *stop* thinking of the people you love. You'll be bringing them to their deaths. *Living* deaths.'

'I know. I couldn't help myself. I wanted to see them, but it was just darkness. My own voice in my head, and darkness. The words fell out of my mouth.' She squeezed Huntley's arm, wished she could feel sensation in her dead fingers. 'How come you could fight it?'

Even in the thick gloom, she caught the look of shame flit across his face. 'I'm useless to these creatures. There's no one I can summon here, no one I'm close to. My parents are dead and I've never…' He looked away. 'Well, my work is very important to me.'

'That's good. That's fantastic,' Rose told him. 'Means you can help me – if I look like I'm going under again, you can pinch me or something. Now, you said there are others who can fight the effect of these things.'

'A few of the *Ascendant* crew,' said Huntley. 'Perhaps because they've been exposed to the effects of these creatures for so long. Come and meet them. I'm hoping we can help others to fight it.' Huntley took her hand, then paused. 'Because the fate that awaits us awaits your loved ones too – the moment you draw them here.'

'Oh, God…' Rose bit her lip as the implications sank in. Then she frowned. 'What d'you mean, "the fate that awaits us"?' She dabbed at the flaps of skin in her neck. 'It can *get* worse than this?'

'Oh, yes. Crayshaw told me. It's almost time for the feast.'

'What does that even mean?'

So he told her, and Rose felt the cold grow deeper and darker inside. Then she followed him in silence, her tears mixing with the dark floodwater of the pit.

'Yes!' Vida cheered as, with a final, desperate blow, the Doctor freed the cleaner's foot from the icy trap. He tossed aside his chunk of concrete and helped her pull herself out. The cleaner lost her trainer in the process, but she reached up for Mickey, who grabbed hold of her hands and yanked her up to the ledge.

Crayshaw, however, was looming closer on his watery platform, arms outstretched.

'Look out, Doctor!' shouted Vida.

The Doctor hurled the trainer at Crayshaw's head. The surprise attack caught the old man off guard. His dark glasses were knocked clear as he twisted and fell backwards, while the Doctor climbed nimbly up the rock pile and rejoined the others.

'I didn't say "shoo",' he panted. 'You know, shoe, shoo, play on words. D'you think I should've said "shoo"?'

'No,' said Mickey.

Vida swallowed hard, pointed. 'Look at Crayshaw.'

He was lying on his front; in the fall, the scarf around his neck had come loose. Something moved, squirming beneath the fabric. Vida caught a glimpse of something bloated and hideous skulking at the top of the old man's spine, a dead, wide eye glistening in a slimy carapace. Then Crayshaw's body and clothes dissolved into water and started flowing sluggishly up the pile of concrete towards them.

'What was that fishy thing?' asked Mickey.

'A glimpse of the real enemy. Probably plugged right into the brain stem for maximum control of the subject. Now come on, help me shift this thing!' The Doctor kicked at one of the larger chunks of concrete that bridged the gap to their vantage point. 'Better try to leave ourselves high and dry.'

Vida hesitated, listening to the frantic shouts for help from the other survivors. 'Those poor people down there won't be able to reach us!'

The Doctor spared her a moment's look, the anguish clear on his face. 'There's nothing we can do for them right now.'

Mickey squeezed in beside him, lent his strength, until the huge slab teetered over and fell to the ice below.

'Don't leave us!' screamed one of the soldiers. But then a wave crashed over him, the water flowing sluggishly, sticking to his face and limbs. A thick split appeared in the ice at his feet as he collapsed. It swallowed him up before he could make another sound. Elsewhere in the labs, the water was churning with fresh fury, knocking over those few still standing. Keeping them under.

Vida looked down. The water flowing up the rock pile towards them had reached the new precipice. It began to hiss and bubble. In a blur, Crayshaw was back, balancing on the rock. She retreated instinctively. Even in human form, he couldn't reach them. But looking at the pitted pearls in his skull-like face, she felt anything but safe here.

'Return Kelper to us,' he said calmly. 'Or we shall destroy Rose Tyler, Andrew Dolan, all of them.'

'Leave Rose alone!' Mickey shouted, starting forwards. But the Doctor held him back.

'You need those people,' the Doctor argued.

Crayshaw shook his head. 'The calling goes on. So many come to answer. The number of victims increases exponentially. Soon the Thames will be choked with bodies, all awaiting our purpose.'

'And what would that be?' the Doctor breathed. 'Just why do you need so much flesh?'

Vida felt sick as an especially nasty penny dropped. 'Doctor, he said that these things are nearing their time to spawn.'

'What?' Mickey turned up his nose. 'You mean those fish things are gonna…'

'Reproduce.' Vida pointed at Kelper, hanging back in the passageway. 'They want him to arrange ships to carry them and their hatchlings away around the world, to start the whole thing over, again and again.'

'Hatchlings. From eggs.' The Doctor stared at him. 'So *that's* why. You need incubators. *Human* incubators. I'm right, aren't I?'

Crayshaw smiled. 'It is the spawning time.'

'Yeah, yeah, and the living is easy. How long have you been on Earth, anyway? How many centuries?'

'We lay dormant for so long, our numbers few, our energy spent from projecting ourselves through space. We recharged, drew energy from the creatures of the sea.'

'And then you got a taste for drowning humans.' The Doctor's eyes were wide and dark. 'Got your teeth into the dominant species. Saved them from death so you could give them something worse.'

'We learned from them. Learned the possibilities of their world, and how we could walk among them.' He stroked one of his ruined eyes. 'Crayshaw was the first. I took his drowning body, his energy and knowledge, made them mine. He became the hive queen.'

'The navy used to frown on that sort of thing, you know.'

Crayshaw ignored him. 'Now it is the spawning time.'

'Lovely. So your biological clock's gone off and here you are, ready to plant your eggs in the locals – once they've been reeled in and turned into suitable carriers, of course.'

'Humans form strong emotional bonds,' said Crayshaw calmly. 'They never stop reaching out to the people they care for, in their thoughts, their dreams...' Then he smiled. 'The images of friends and loved ones are so clear in their minds. Sharpened by longing, by despair, by the craving for contact. We simply reach out to those people.'

The Doctor looked at him coldly. 'I've come across some twisted, cynical, *brutal* schemes in my time. But to get your grubby little flippers on love and passion and grief and turn them into *fishing hooks*...'

'We require strong emotions and the data they carry. They aid our purpose.'

'Oh yeah, your purpose. Let me see if I got that right.' The Doctor clenched his hands into fists. 'You make the Thames into a paddock for your underwater cattle. And once the eggs hatch inside them, the newborn devour the flesh from the inside. A right old nosh-up. Yum-yum, pig's bum. A proper feast.'

'The feast of the drowned,' Mickey whispered. 'That's what the ghosts were going on about.'

The Doctor put on a posh voice. 'Will all loved ones kindly assemble beneath the Thames before the feast – so they can become a part of it.'

'The hatchlings must feed,' said Crayshaw. 'The waterhive must spread.'

'Not at this cost!' the Doctor shouted. 'You'll be slaughtering millions all over the planet.'

'Why is he letting us work all this out?' said Vida sharply. Then she saw the dribbles of water creeping up the tiled wall, almost level with the precipice. 'Doctor!'

The Doctor whirled round, pointed the screwdriver. With a scream of ultrasonics the wall gave way beside them. The vibration almost knocked Vida off her feet, but Mickey grabbed hold of her, stopped her from falling.

But the water had been climbing on the other side of their hole in the wall too. The Doctor jerked round with his device a fraction too late – Commodore Powers ghosted into existence and smacked it from his grip. Before any of them could react, he had grabbed the Doctor by the throat.

Then, in a blur of movement, the cleaner charged in and kicked Powers in the stomach. He staggered back, dragging the Doctor with him. Both were about to go over the edge, but Mickey grabbed hold of one arm and Vida lunged for the other, pulling the Doctor clear. Powers let go and hit the rubble-strewn floor with a splash, dissolving into nothing, clothes and all.

The cleaner was fuming. 'They can stick their job!'

The Doctor righted himself, turned and dropped a kiss on the cleaner's head. 'Thank you.' He leaned back over the precipice and bellowed down to the churning water below, 'Let me tell you *my* purpose. I'm going to stop you. Whatever it takes.' Then he beamed at Mickey and Vida as he picked up his screwdriver and strode backwards away from the ledge, into the gloomy quiet of the tunnel where Jodie North was still waiting.

And once there, his brave face dropped like a ton of bricks. 'Think they believed me?'

Nobody spoke. The only sound was the water, roaring round the ruined lab like an angry hunter cheated of its kill.

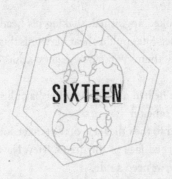

SIXTEEN

Keisha had hold of Jackie's hand and was pulling her through the thronging streets. They had met the first soldiers some way from the river. The checkpoint blocking the road was one of scores that had brought traffic to a standstill, as drivers were forced to divert down all manner of back streets and one-way systems.

There was more than just annoyance in the eyes of some of these passers-by. She saw despair, anger, determination. How many of them were looking for a way through to the river?

Now they were looking for a new route in, and round the corner one City gent thought he might have found an ally. He was shouting at the driver of a tanker, banging his fist on the door. 'Take me with you! I need to get to my daughter!'

'You're crazy.'

'Come on, we can smash the roadblocks in that!'

'I'm not even going to the river!'

Keisha didn't believe the driver either. Maybe she would have more luck where the man had failed. She was about to go over when she saw Jay, there in the middle of the unseeing crowd. He looked anguished, shaking his head, holding out his hands to her. She couldn't hear his words this time, but she could imagine them: *Why're you waiting, Keish? Time's running out.*

Even before he had melted away, Keisha pulled Jackie along behind her. 'Come on.'

She ran over to the other side of the tanker, looked up at the angry, sunburned face of the driver. 'Hey. Never mind him. Jackie and me, *we* need a ride.'

The driver hesitated for just a few seconds. 'All right. But your mum stays in the back –' Suddenly he shut his eyes, fell forwards. The next thing Keisha knew, the door flew open and he fell to the pavement at her feet.

Jackie was down and fussing straight away. 'You all right?' she said, and looked up at Keisha. 'He's been hit from behind.'

The City gent swung himself into the driver's seat. 'Get in if you want to. They'll never stop us in this.'

'You're going to the river, then?' Jackie asked.

'Of course,' he said. 'I've got to get to my daughter before the feast.'

Keisha rushed straight round to the other side of the cab and yanked open the door. *At last,* she thought. *No more fretting or thinking or arguing. You can do this.*

Jay, Rose. I'm coming.

Rose moved slowly through the eerie ranks of the drowned. They milled about in the thick water, the dull gleam of their silvery eyes the only light, their hair drifting lazily in the water like weeds. Anne must be here somewhere, gills cut into her kindly face. Poor old PC Fraser too, together with his mate at last. And how many others had they unwittingly summoned here in turn?

The anger Rose felt was as cold as the rest of her. *Don't think about Mum*, she told herself. *And whatever you do, don't think about...*

Him.

Huntley led her to where six or seven people huddled together in naval uniform. They had to have come from the *Ascendant*. Then Rose's heart twitched as she recognised one dark, hunched figure sat with his head in hands. 'Jay!' She crouched beside him, took him by the shoulders. 'Jay, it's me, Rose.'

He saw her and smiled sadly. 'I tried so hard not to bring you here.'

'You didn't. I got myself into this.' She closed her eyes for a minute, feeling dizzy. 'And we're the only ones who can get ourselves out of it.'

'I tried to escape,' Jay told her. 'They brought me back.'

'Then we'll try again.'

'They know when we've gone.'

'There are more of us now. Maybe we can fight back.'

Jay clutched at Rose's arm. 'I could see Keish this time. Couldn't make myself heard, but I could see her.' He looked at her. 'She's with your mum – and they're coming.'

Vida was still huddling with the others in the shattered section of the tunnel when she realised one of their party was missing. 'What happened to Kelper?'

'The admiral guy went up there,' said Jodie, pointing her gun up the shadowy tunnel.

'How well do you and your boss know him, Vida?' the Doctor asked.

'Mainly through phone calls and email. I'd never met him in the flesh till today, and Andrew's only seen him through video-conferencing.'

'Good. No strong emotional data for the hive to attack him through Andrew. If they want to get him they'll have to follow him through those conduits. Should buy us some time.' He rubbed his hands briskly together. 'Well, chat with the enemy accomplished, anyway. Big tick. We know a bit more than we did before.'

'It's horrible.' Mickey looked ready to tear his hair out. 'I mean… *eggs*? They haven't just drowned Rose, they've turned her into walking caviar!'

Vida chewed her lip. 'Will they really kill her?' She paused. 'And Andrew?'

The Doctor shook his head. 'I don't think so. Destroy the eggs inside their bodies out of spite? Not very productive. And productivity's what hives are all about.'

'But if those eggs hatch…' Mickey broke off, shuddering.

'*When* they hatch,' the Doctor corrected him bleakly. 'The hive will just keep on growing. We're dealing with a shared hive consciousness that connects through water molecules.' He shook his head in apparent admiration. 'What a mind! How incredible is that!'

'How can they hope to stay hidden if it's all gonna kick off in the Thames? The rest of the country will see what's happening, get its act together, wipe them out.'

'This is only the start,' Vida told him. 'Commodore Powers might already have arranged transport of these monsters to other key bases. And if they get hold of Kelper, they can start hitching rides in the US navy fleet, conquer America…'

'Your species might start twigging in the end,' said the Doctor softly. 'Once millions have died to become fish food, and millions more from dehydration. But by then they'll be ready to move on to the next world.'

'How?' Vida demanded. 'Little fishy spaceships?'

'Water's their medium. They probably project themselves through space using mental power. Plenty of H_2 in space, they could power-fuse it with oxygen…'

'Wait,' hissed Jodie North, levelling her gun. 'Movement. Back there.'

Vida waited expectantly, held her breath.

'It's me.' Kelper appeared out of the shadows. 'I was… scouting out the area.'

The Doctor sighed. 'You got lost, didn't you?'

'I take it these conduits lead back to the surface eventually?' he asked stonily. 'I must get to someone in authority. We need to wipe out these things.'

'How about you shut up a minute?' the Doctor snapped. 'What you need to do is to get organising some ships to seal off the Thames. Countermand any order that's been given by Commodore Powers – he's one of them. No ship is to leave for open sea under any circumstances – got it?'

'But I'm US navy,' he protested, 'it'll take time to arrange –'

'*Make it happen!*' the Doctor thundered. 'Now, move!'

Vida interceded. 'It's OK, you can trust him.'

'Go about 300 feet up this tunnel, then right, left, up a bit, left, straight on at the junction, a right…' The Doctor paused, frowned at Kelper. 'You getting this?'

'*I* am,' said the cleaner breathlessly. 'My boyfriend drives a cab. It rubs off on you.'

The Doctor gave her a rakish smile. 'You're just perfect, you are. So, like I was saying – a right, and then straight on till you reach the hard-hat cupboard at Aldgate station.' He lowered his voice, nodded confidentially at Kelper. 'Oh, and look after the bloke in the braid. Apparently he's important. You'll be targets.' He patted Jodie North on the back. 'Go with them too.'

She swung her gun on to her shoulder, but she looked uncertain. 'Protection?'

'Safety in numbers.'

'What about you?'

'Just get going.'

'No, hang on, she's got a point,' said Mickey. 'What about us, what *are* we gonna do? And what about Rose? It won't take those things long to figure out a way of getting up here, will it?'

Jodie hesitated, reached into a pouch in her uniform and pulled out two chunky grenades. 'Bullets were no good. Maybe I should have tried these.' She pressed one into each of the Doctor's hands. He stared at them, bemused, as if it was Christmas and she was handing him Easter eggs.

'Whoa,' said Vida. 'Bit heavy for a security job, aren't they?'

'Crayshaw's orders,' said Jodie.

'He believes in being prepared,' the Doctor observed. 'Ta, Jodie, but no ta. I could never use these.'

'I could!' Mickey gingerly took the grenades himself. 'Not even you can talk everything to death.'

'It's a five-second fuse. Thumb down on the safety lever, yank out the pin and throw it as far as you can.'

'What, the pin?' inquired the Doctor politely.

'The grenade. The fragments are dangerous up to 150 feet.'

'That's if we don't bring the whole tunnel down on our heads,' Vida said.

The cleaner was already hauling Kelper away. 'Come on, then!'

'Good luck,' said Jodie, and soon she had vanished down the narrow tunnel.

'Now, then.' The Doctor yanked out a thick, heavy-duty cable from the shattered wall of the conduit, and crossed it with another couple of exposed wires.

'What're you doing?' asked Mickey.

'Most of Secret London's emergency power supply runs through here, and water's a brilliant conductor.' A vivid crackle of electricity sparked from the cable, and the Doctor let go hastily. 'There. Should give anything that tries to follow the vice admiral and his friends a bit of a shock.'

Vida sucked in her cheeks. 'Do you think that will stop them for long?'

'Not really.' He had already set off further along the tunnel, which sloped downwards at an alarming angle. 'Let's just hope that when they get going, they come after us and not Kelper. After all, now that Mickey the untrained civilian's got a couple of hand grenades in his pockets, hey! We're safe as houses!'

'Yes,' sighed Vida. 'Aren't we just.'

'Oh, Mum…' Rose felt herself starting to panic at the thought she might bring her here. 'No. I mustn't think of her.' She tried to shut off her thoughts, pictured the TARDIS standing between them (as it usually did), blocking her view. Yes, the TARDIS was a good thing to think about, it was sort of soothing. Patient, strong and blue…

'Better?' Huntley asked her quietly.

'Yeah.' But her new-found anchor threatened to take off again, sharpish, as another thought suddenly hit her. 'Hang on. Jay, what d'you mean, you've *seen* them?'

'I tried to warn Keish away, but…' Jay strained, and she saw dark blood cloud out from his swollen eyelid. 'This stuff in me wouldn't let the words out.'

'But you could actually *see* her and my mum? Through the eyes of your image?'

Huntley crouched down beside them, nodding knowledgeably. 'This interests me hugely. The aquatic intelligence must still be using his mind to track its victims and project an apparition – but now Jay and some of these others report a degree of control over what the apparition says when it arrives. Maybe because they've been here longer than the rest of us, their body's mutating cells are –'

'Yeah, well, never mind how and why.' Rose felt so tired suddenly. 'The point is, if he can do it maybe we *all* can.'

'I'm not giving up,' Jay insisted.

'And neither will we,' said Rose. She looked at Huntley. 'Just imagine if we *could* do it – we could play these creatures at their own game! Confuse their message, get our own ones through.'

But even as she said it, Rose doubled up with pain, clutching her temples. It felt as if something was dragging itself out of her head. Huntley grabbed hold of her, but she could barely focus.

The TARDIS in her head disappeared. But it wasn't her mum she saw clearly now…

Mickey held aside a fat bundle of wires so the Doctor could do his sonic stuff on the tunnel wall. It was supposed to be a safe place to break through, into a kind of basement beneath the labs. Which was cool. So long as you tried not to think about the tons of earth and concrete between you and a sniff of fresh air, or that you were a good half-mile from any idea of safety…

And after all Vida had told them on the way about her night in Crayshaw's company, Mickey couldn't imagine feeling safe ever again. He looked at her. 'What I don't get is how come you weren't given the gills and pearls treatment straight away, like Rose and your boss.'

She shrugged. 'Cosmetic reasons, I suppose. I was meant to lure Kelper here. None of us realised he'd arrived here under his own steam. Crayshaw was ready to drown us once he had everyone together. If you hadn't turned up…'

'Got to be more than that, though, hasn't it?' The Doctor had his ear pressed against the concrete like a safecracker trying to crack the combination. 'I mean, yeah, it was handy to have you about to lure the vice admiral here. But they went to a lot of trouble to kidnap you and take you back to Stanchion House. Yesterday evening, Crayshaw wasn't bothered if you were killed while helping me escape.'

'He knew that we'd taken samples from the sea, that we knew of these things' existence.' She rubbed her tired eyes. 'You thought earlier that they might be after our new tracers, to use as a weapon.'

'That was before we knew what they were really up to...' He switched off the screwdriver for a moment, a gobsmacked expression spreading over his face. 'Oh, now hang on a sec...'

Mickey started choking. 'My mouth's gone dry.'

'Mine too,' hissed Vida.

'Stop it, Doctor!' Rose glowed into sudden ghostly existence right in front of them, cold and grey as the sea. 'You mustn't interfere. They'll kill me if you do.'

'Rose!' Mickey shouted out and collapsed, clutching his legs.

Water poured from the spectre's eyes. 'They'll destroy me!'

'You're destroying them!' the Doctor shouted back. 'Listen to me, Mickey, Vida. Whatever you're seeing, you mustn't believe it. Shut it out.'

'Can't,' croaked Mickey, staring transfixed.

Vida felt her insides ache and burn, wanted to cry but no tears would come.

'Rose, remember what I told you,' the Doctor implored the vision. 'We trust the people we love to tell the truth. We trust them not to harm us.'

'What's she doing?' gasped Vida.

'The apparition is strengthening itself with the water from your bodies.' The Doctor clutched hold of Mickey's hand, pressed his forehead up close to Vida's. 'You *must* shut it out!'

An enormous, crushing blackness was bulldozing through Vida's head. But she could still hear the sound of Rose's voice.

'Don't fight, Doctor,' said the voice. 'Surrender to us. Or your friends will die.'

SEVENTEEN

'Fight it, Rose!' Huntley was yelling in her face. How come the water didn't deaden the sound? 'Come on, fight it!'

Rose heard him but couldn't reply. Her brain felt so hot, the water around her should have been bubbling.

Then she was aware of strong arms round her waist, and heard Jay's voice in her ear. 'Go with it, Rose. Go into the image. Open its eyes and look through them.'

Jay was cuddling her. How many nights had fourteen-year-old Rose Tyler spent awake dreaming of this? She felt a sudden contented glow inside her. A glow that grew brighter, white-hot, like the supernatural shine at the centre of the TARDIS. She closed her eyes, but somehow that made the light brighter still, so she opened them again.

And suddenly she could see Mickey on the ground in some poky little hole, and the Doctor, wide-eyed and fierce and desperate, while Vida was reaching out to someone else Rose couldn't see, racked with pain.

We trust the people we love to tell the truth.

'Stop… hurting…' she said. 'Just stop…'

* * *

'...*hurting* them.'

Vida felt the blackness beginning to clear, saw that the image of Rose was losing form and focus.

'You what?' The Doctor started nodding encouragingly at the phantom. 'Rose, say again!'

'Doctor! Forget about me, just stop these –'

The image burst into droplets and vanished. Vida felt sick. Her head ached, but she was alive.

'What happened?' asked Mickey, pushing himself up off the floor.

'Grenade no good, then, Mickey? Fancy that!'

Either he ignored the jibe or it didn't register. 'I thought I was being squeezed out, like a sponge...'

'Rose tried to put back what she took,' said the Doctor. 'She fought the hive influence. Hijacked the apparition and used it to communicate with us...'

Vida felt slow and unsteady. 'How?'

'Maybe she had help. Maybe the waterhive's influence is being spread thinner as its victims rack up. Maybe it's because her travels with me have affected her body's make-up in some way...' He shrugged and smiled to himself. 'Or maybe just because she's Rose.'

'You were right,' said Vida. 'Assistants can come in very useful.' Mickey had pulled a small bottle of water from his pocket. He offered her a swig and she accepted it gratefully. 'I'm just glad they didn't send Andrew in against me.'

'It's me they see as the threat. So they used someone known to all three of us.'

'Will they try again?'

'They might not know they've failed,' said the Doctor cautiously. 'Her image cut out – could be the aquatic equivalent of a blown fuse in their neural network. They'll need to try and fix it, which might buy us some time.'

'I suppose it shows that these creatures aren't completely unbeatable.'

'You've done pretty well at proving that, Vida,' said Mickey. 'They try to shoot you while escaping with him, and you escape. They try to kidnap you and drag you back here, and you escape.'

The Doctor got to work with his sonic screwdriver again. 'Good point, Mickey.'

'What?'

'Their attitude to Vida, like I said, hasn't been all that consistent, has it? The waterhive went to a lot of time and trouble spiriting you away from your offices. Why?'

Vida frowned. 'Just unlucky, I suppose.'

'No!' he shouted. 'It's because of me and what I got up to in your labs! That sample of water from the drainage pit – I must have made it shout for help.'

Vida was far too tired and scared to be offended. 'So Crayshaw's minions came running, thinking that since *I* work there, it's me who's doing it.'

'They didn't know any better. Their water tried to get inside my head, but it couldn't.' He licked a finger and smoothed one eyebrow. 'My God, I'm just too good.'

'So what were you doing to that water?' Mickey demanded.

'Vida, you know, those subatomic filaments you were hoping to release from the *Ascendant*, those tiny transmitters and receivers?' His face was lit creepily in the blue glow from the screwdriver. 'I'd just mixed some into the alien water to see what happened.'

'And what *did* happen?'

'Nothing. Bit of a disappointment, really.'

'How d'you know it was nothing? You didn't have the gear to pick up the filaments' signals.'

'I know. But the water didn't seem to care. No frothing, no churning, no bubbling over, nothing…' He froze. 'Nothing. Nothing?' He yanked down hard on the housing of the screwdriver, made it flare into bright blue life. '*Nothing!*'

And then the wall exploded. Vida threw herself backwards into Mickey as the three of them were peppered with chips of concrete.

'That's a pretty big kind of nothing,' Mickey choked, as Vida helped him back up.

'And so was that nothing in the water,' the Doctor crowed, waving his arm about to dispel some of the thick concrete dust. 'The hive didn't want those tracers to use as a weapon. It didn't want *us* to have them – in case *we* used them as a weapon!'

Vida stared at him. 'You mean that something in the tracers can stop the flow of the hive consciousness, mess up the apparitions, the flow of commands…'

He nodded, grinning broadly. 'But it's better than that! Rose has just proved that the alien signals can be *overridden*. That the human voice can still be heard. If we could somehow use the transmitters in the tracers to amplify that effect, we could stuff these creatures *right* up! I'm sure we could!'

Mickey was smiling too, bless him, caught up in the moment. 'And so, we've got some of these tracer things, right?'

The Doctor pulled a face. 'Er… Not as such.'

Mickey closed his eyes, seemed to shrink. 'Then *we're* the ones who are stuffed.'

'I know where we can get some,' Vida announced, almost reluctantly. 'But how the hell would we activate them?'

'Never mind that.' The Doctor grabbed her by the waist. 'Where? Where are they?'

She shrugged. 'We had a great big batch of them stowed aboard the *Ascendant*, remember? It went down before they could be released into the ocean.'

Mickey jerked a weary thumb over his shoulder, pointing back the way they had come. 'That would be the *Ascendant* lying in pieces back there?'

The Doctor waved him into silence. 'Do you know where they were stored?'

'I was there this morning. The ship's stores, where Crayshaw had his gloat over me. Still on board the cargo trailer.'

'Oh, t'riffic,' said Mickey. 'So basically, we're stuck way down here, about as far underground as it's possible to be, while the stuff we need is floating on top of the river.'

'Looks like it,' the Doctor agreed, his eyes darting all around. You could almost hear his mind working its way through a million mad strategies. 'Still, look on the bright side, Mickey.' He flashed a small but dangerous smile. 'For you, the only way is up!'

* * *

'I did it,' Rose breathed. She was slumped on the floor, numb all over from the freezing water, but something fierce and satisfied burned inside her.

'What happened?' asked Jay. She realised he was squeezing her hand.

'I saw my friends. Spoke to them – just for a minute.' She struggled up. 'It was so hard, though.'

Jay looked up at Huntley. 'How come I can't do it?'

'I had an unfair advantage,' said Rose. 'I think… I think maybe the TARDIS gave me a bit of a push.'

Huntley raised an eyebrow. 'The what?'

'Doesn't matter.'

'Rose, can you talk to Keish?' Jay asked urgently.

'I can try,' she told him, squeezing his hand back.

High up in the cab of the tanker, Keisha stared out calmly at the nightmare London had become. Crowds of people were swarming through the streets as if led by an invisible Pied Piper, anxious and determined. They surged up to the blockades that barred all access to the Thames, shouting and screaming to be let through. Sometimes the army fired shots in the air, trying to scare them back, but the crowd barely reacted.

Keisha understood these people. They were on a mission to save the ones they loved, and so was she.

Jackie sat to her left, the gent driving to her right. He was pale and sweaty, stinking out the cab, gripping the wheel so tightly that his knuckles shone white. 'We can't let these people hold us up any longer,' he said, and revved the powerful engine. 'If we drive on the pavement we can reach that barrier, smash straight through. A bus got through last night – we should try it.'

'But there are all these people in the way,' said Jackie distantly.

'My Nicky needs me,' the driver said.

'Maybe if you honk the horn,' Keisha suggested.

'What, and warn the soldiers? They'll shoot us!' He revved the engine again, shut his eyes, like he was psyching himself up. 'No, it has to be this way. You can see that, can't you?'

But all Keisha could see was Rose. Her friend was floating in front of her like a ghost. She looked terrible. Her face was scored with bloody lines. Her eyes were all wrong – silvery, smooth, no pupils. Keisha opened her mouth to cry out but Jackie was already lunging forwards, as if she could grasp the vision's hands.

'Oh, my God, Rose, sweetheart, we're coming!'

'No, Mum!' Rose shouted. 'It's… a trick. Evil. You've got to stop…'

'But Rose!'

'Keish? Jay's safe. But he won't be if you come.' She gritted her teeth. 'Whatever you see, keep everyone back… away from here… Get me?'

Keisha wiped away her tears. 'What can we do?'

'We're sorting it.' She closed her eyes, pressed her face against the windscreen. Jackie reached out a trembling hand to the glass.

But then the image was gone, just water on the windscreen blurring their view of the chaos outside.

'I've got to get to Nicky,' the man shouted, revving the engine. His hand shook as he shoved the tanker into first gear. 'Nothing else matters.'

The huge lorry lurched towards the crowd like a giant dog straining at the leash.

And Jackie punched out the driver with a single blow to the jaw. His feet slipped from the pedals and the lorry choked and stalled.

'Didn't you hear my Rose?' she snapped, rubbing her fist, though her knuckles weren't as red as her eyes. 'It's a *trick*.'

'What were we doing?' Keisha whispered, trembling. 'What were we *gonna* do?'

Jackie pulled her in for a frightened hug as more gunshots were fired off above the rioting crowd. 'And what are we going to do now?'

Mickey pelted up the emergency stairs, Vida close behind. The Doctor had sent them through on their own while he doubled back the other way. He was the main target, so he figured there was a better chance of them making it up and out of the building without him.

'I'll try to draw their fire,' he'd said, disappearing through the hole in the wall into the gloom of the basement. 'Well, their water, anyway. In a manner of speaking.'

There was a clanky-looking service lift in the basement area. Vida had the smart idea of sending it right up to the top floor while they took the emergency steps to Ground. 'That way, if they hear the lift going, they'll get busy laying an ambush for us – while we walk out of the front door.'

It had sounded great in theory. But there were so many steps!

'Let's rest,' said Vida, leaning against the stair-rail.

Mickey nodded, tugging at his T-shirt, which was damp with sweat. 'Only for a sec, though,' he said. 'The lift must have reached the top floor by now.'

'That's not the only thing that's bothering me,' said Vida.

'Oh?'

'Even assuming the tracers weren't destroyed in the wreck of the *Ascendant*, and even assuming we can get our hands on them. How do we deploy them?'

'How do we what?'

'There are, what, 4,500 million gallons of water in the Thames, right?'

Mickey frowned. 'I've gone metric, I'll take your word for it.'

Vida ignored him. 'And with the average current, what... three knots max? It's going to take time to disperse them – even if we had a transmitter to set them off, which we don't. Even if we knew what the Doctor had in mind –'

'Which we don't,' Mickey agreed. 'But he's done this world-saving stuff before. It's best just to go –'

'With the flow?' Vida shuddered. 'Come on, then. We haven't got much further to go.' She pushed off again. 'Another few flights.'

But as she spoke there was an echoing clang from somewhere down below, as if a fire door had been flung open.

Quickly followed by the sound of rushing water.

Mickey peered over the edge of the handrail and saw dark, frothing fluid surging up the steps, just a few turns of the staircase behind them. 'Leg it!' he yelled.

He pushed himself to speed up, taking the steps two, three at a time, his legs buzzing with pins and needles. His throat burned with thirst, but he guessed copping a mouthful of intelligent water wouldn't make him feel much better.

Vida was starting to lag behind. He paused for just a moment, offered his hand. She took it and they set off again, silent as they ran, forcing themselves to move faster and faster. Because the water was gaining on them now; it was splashing against the walls as it thundered up, churning and gurgling.

Finally they reached the top of the stairwell. A formidable metal door was set into the concrete. 'Please don't let it be locked,' gasped Vida.

Mickey tugged on it. It *was* locked. 'You still got soldier-girl's passcard?'

'I don't know!' She scrabbled at the pockets of her dusty black trousers as the water crashed noisily around another corner, not far behind them now. 'Got it!' She jammed it into the slot beside the heavy door.

A small red light started winking on the card-reader, like an obscene gesture.

'What's wrong with it?' panted Mickey.

'Don't tell me she's not got access to this level,' Vida wailed.

She pulled out the card and shoved it in again, beat a fist on the door in frustration as the water tore round the final concrete corner and gushed up the steps towards them.

'I did all I could,' Rose told Jay. 'I think I got through to them, but I don't know...' She blew out an underwater sigh. 'It's crazy up there. In fact –' she stood up shakily – 'I think we need to go there ourselves. To the surface.'

'That's twice you've played against their rules,' Huntley warned her. 'They could be on to you now.'

Rose bit her lip. 'Then I'll keep them busy while you escape.'

'Escape? But...' Huntley dithered. 'Can we still breathe air?'

'It's hard, but I did it,' said Jay. 'The waterway to the river was guarded, so I tried the cargo lift shaft. Managed to get all the way up. But I was too slow. They found me, took me back.'

Rose nodded. 'The Doctor saw you, he tried to help.'

'And now there are guards making sure no one else has a go,' Jay concluded.

'The tug's gone anyway,' said Rose. 'So no escape that way. We'll just have to leave the same way we came in.'

'But the guards!' Huntley protested. 'Surely –'

'They might know that I've been causing trouble, but not the rest of you,' Rose told him. 'If we can only get out of here, show people what's happened to us, tell them how they're being tricked.' Huntley still looked unsure. 'What have we got to lose? We're full of alien eggs that could hatch any minute!'

'There's nothing to lose,' Jay agreed, and Huntley reluctantly nodded.

'Then round up the boys, boys,' said Rose. 'We're busting out of here.'

'Come on!' Mickey shouted. He glanced back at the filthy tide coming to drown them, pulled out one of the grenades. 'Should I let this off, try and knock out the stairs?'

'Hang on.' Vida wiped the card on her sleeve and shoved it in again. The rush of water seemed to gather itself like a vast cobra, ready to strike.

And finally the card-reader winked green. 'Yes!' yelled Mickey.

Vida flung open the door and piled through. Mickey followed her and slammed the door shut behind them. They pelted along a corridor, through some more double doors, along another corridor...

'Where's the way out?' shouted Mickey.

'Keep going!' Vida yelled back.

But behind them came a savage splintering noise as the stairwell door was torn from its hinges by the great rush of water. Seconds later, with a stereo crash, the double doors were thrown open. The hissing, bubbling sound rushed closer and closer.

'We can't outrun it,' shouted Vida as they stumbled into the main reception at last.

'Remember Crayshaw down there?' Mickey scrambled up on to the reception desk, pulled her up after him. 'Old sea dog. New tricks.'

The tide of dirty water smashed through into reception, the stairwell door pitching on top of it like a massive surfboard. Mickey nodded to Vida and jumped for it –

Don't mess up, don't mess up, don't mess –

He landed awkwardly, fell to his knees, dropped the grenade and swore. But at least he was on board, and Vida was clinging on behind him. She shrieked and he yelled as the miniature tsunami reared up, carrying them above the turnstiles.

And straight into the plate-glass frontage of Stanchion House.

The door hit the thick glass edge-on and shattered it. Mickey twisted round so his back took the impact, fell forwards on to Vida. For a second the two clung together as jagged shards rained down around them. Then their makeshift bodyboard hit the ground and Mickey was thrown clear. He rolled over and over –

He must have blacked out for a minute. Next thing he knew Vida was cradling him on the ground and there was blood on the sleeve of his T-shirt. Hers or his? He hurt everywhere *except* his arm, so maybe it was hers.

'Did we make it?' he asked, staring round, head spinning.

'Almost,' she told him softly.

And as his vision focussed he saw the pirate, the Victorian lady and the kid, all looming over him. Their heads looked too big for their bodies, the faces bloated and eel-white, misshapen eyes ready to plop out of their sockets as they reached down to tear at him with shrivelled, groping fingers.

EIGHTEEN

'Coo-ee?' The Doctor, all set for a diversion, peeped through the hole he had made in the wall of the underground laboratories. They had been trashed and deserted. Plastic partitions lay in crumpled heaps and big cracks had opened in the floor and walls where bits of ship had toppled over. It was eerily quiet.

'O ye whales, and all who move in the waters!' he loudly declaimed, smiling despite himself at the richness of the echoes that bounced back at him. 'Here, fishy fishy!' The whiff of burning plastic in the conduit told him his trap with the electric cable had been sprung and overcome. But where were Crayshaw and company now?

Answer: right in front of him.

Water gushed out of one of the cracks in the floor, and Crayshaw formed from the foam, scarf and dark glasses back in place. 'Why have you returned?'

'Like the humans you're manipulating, I couldn't stay away. Caught up with Kelper yet?'

'He will soon be recaptured.'

'If not, it sets back your plans for expansion, doesn't it? You need the ships he can arrange for you. You need –' The Doctor broke off, distracted by Crayshaw's specs and shawl. 'Look, why are you still bothering to hide behind those? No, don't tell me. I suppose after all these years it's harder *not* to assemble the accoutrements out of thin air like that.'

'Not from thin air. From the constituent atoms of the original.'

'That's probably very clever, but you make it sound so *boring!*' He tutted sadly. 'That's the trouble with you hive minds. No imagination. Dull as ditchwater.' He frowned. 'Sorry, I hope ditchwater isn't a close personal friend of yours.'

Suddenly the bloated corpses of two fishermen appeared, grabbed an arm each and twisted. The Doctor shouted in pain, didn't struggle.

'Your friends are attempting to escape,' Crayshaw informed him.

'You know, they're always doing things like that.'

'They will not succeed.'

'Really? That's a pity.' He tried to shrug, though his arms were pinned behind his back. 'Humans, eh? Aren't they annoying? You think they're under your control, when they suddenly shuck off your mental dominance, demonstrate free will, start hijacking your pheromonal images to get their own messages across…'

'Occasional aberrations are inevitable,' said Crayshaw, 'and can be corrected.'

'Aberrations like me?' He nodded. 'You know I'm not human, your watery scout told you that. I imagine that's why you're tolerating a banal conversation like this when you're about to become a mummy several billion times over. You're looking at me and you're thinking – what's he up to? He's resisted us in the past. Why's he handing himself over on a plate?'

'Why have you returned?' Crayshaw asked again.

'To deal. Like I said earlier – no Kelper, no ships, no expansion.' He half-smiled. 'But I have an amazing ship, and powers that are frankly godlike. I'll share these with you – if you leave the Earth and its people alone.'

Crayshaw stood impassive and blank.

'Come on,' the Doctor complained, 'this is a top offer, *amazing* value! I can take you to rich and distant worlds you could never reach under your own steam. Through me the hive can spread not only through space, but through time.' He raised his eyebrows. 'So – *can* I deal with you?'

Suddenly the scarf around Crayshaw's neck started to twitch. His flesh melted away like wrinkled wax to reveal the true creature controlling the old, stiff body.

'Well, well,' said the Doctor. 'The hive queen is an ancient one-eyed eel the size of a Chihuahua.' He sneered at the creature as it sat there, pulsing, watching him with its baleful eye. 'No wonder you prefer a human body.'

'To take these forms is unpleasant to us.'

'But necessary to fool the locals and administer discipline now and then,' the Doctor suggested. 'Go on, be honest – you and your guards just like swanking around in posh bodies while the rest of the hive does its impression of soluble aspirin…'

He trailed off. The queen was twitching, swelling up, her glutinous body growing bigger and fatter. Her eye bulged from behind thickly veined lids. Stubby fins and protuberances squeezed from her vile body like pus from a zit. The quivering mandibles above the gaping 'O' of her mouth straightened and sharpened to evil points. Soon the creature had swollen to the size of a small car.

'I suppose you do that to intimidate your prey,' the Doctor said softly. 'It's very good. Very effective.'

'You wish to share your powers and your ship with me,' hissed the queen. 'I wish to *take* them.'

Held helpless in the grip of her guards, the Doctor could only watch as the terrifying creature slithered towards him.

Vida shut her eyes as the hands came down for them. *We so nearly made it*, she thought, *came so close*. But now it was over. The sound of sirens and shouting carried from the other side of the river, and she bellowed back, in fear and pain and anger that these things would get away with –

'Stop!' came a familiar voice. 'Leave them alone or – or *I* get it!'

Vida's heart jumped in her bruised chest. She looked up, past their gruesome pursuers, and saw Rose in the dripping grip of a bald, portly man in a stained white coat. Hadn't she seen him somewhere before? With a sick feeling she took in the bloody lines scored in the flesh of their cheeks and necks, the pearly tinge to the eyes. And behind them she realised a menagerie of figures in naval uniform, horribly disfigured, was shambling closer.

'Look out, Rose!' she yelled.

'S'all right, they're on our side,' Rose told her. 'Couldn't have got past the guards without them. So, hear this, you water zombie things. Get away from those two people or I'm history – and so are the eggs I'm carrying. Professor Huntley here will kill me!' She gestured behind her. 'And this lot will kill each other too, just watch them!'

Huntley – yes, that was it, one of the secret scientists from downstairs. Vida saw that he had picked up a large chunk of broken glass and was holding it to the girl's neck.

'Get your hands off her,' said Mickey hoarsely. He tried weakly to stand, but Vida shushed him.

'Don't,' she whispered. 'Look, they're doing as she says!' To her astonishment, the three guards were backing uneasily away.

'It's working, they're confused!' Huntley seemed to be having difficulty catching his breath as he called over to them. 'Their instinct is to protect their eggs, as it is in any hive!'

Rose widened her eyes at Mickey and Vida. 'Get over here, then!'

Vida helped Mickey get back up, and they limped warily over to join this bizarre cavalry. 'Where'd you spring from?' she asked.

'Big dark hole in the ground, flooded with water.' But Rose was looking at Mickey as she spoke, her eyes glistening. 'It's bad, isn't it? I look disgusting, don't I?'

Mickey shook his head. 'You don't. You could never.'

She almost smiled. 'Don't lie!'

'I'm not!' he protested, dabbing at a cut above one eye.

'Anyway, the Doctor will fix you up.'

'Where is he?'

Mickey hesitated.

'Mickey, where *is* he?'

He looked as if he wanted to hug her, but Huntley waggled the blade of glass with a meaningful nod at the fancy-dress monsters. Or rather, monster. Vida saw that the pirate and the kid had disappeared, leaving only the Victorian lady giving them the evil pearl eye.

'They've gone to ask Mum what they should do,' Vida surmised. 'We can't have long.'

Now Rose was targeting her. 'Where's the Doctor, Vida?'

'He went to distract Crayshaw, the leader of the hive. To buy us time so we can get the tracers.'

'What, those chemical things you chuck in the ocean?'

'As summaries of my life's work go, that's not bad,' said Vida wryly. 'The Doctor needs us to get those chemical things you chuck in the ocean, but…' She pointed to the cargo dump left behind when they'd taken the tug. 'They should be somewhere in the store lockers. The place you were brought to acclimatise after they… did that to you. Do you remember?'

'Oh yeah,' said Rose, shivering in the sunlight. 'So basically, if we can get past the walking drowned and the sea monsters, we're laughing. What do these tracers look like?'

'Big metal flasks racked in a kind of posh crate,' rasped one of the sailors, a dark-skinned boy. 'There were 100 aboard.'

Vida stared. 'How did you –'

'I worked in the stores,' he told her, wheezing for breath. 'I don't know how many survived the wreck... Maybe none at all. But I'll see what I can find.'

'We'll need the whole crate,' Vida said. 'It's part of the release assembly. It'll take two to shift it, minimum.'

'I'll go with you, Jay,' Rose told him.

'Can't you just stay here?' Mickey urged her.

'What, here where it's safe you mean?' She tapped Huntley on the arm, angled her head back to look at him. 'That's really good threatening, professor, but could you try it on one of the others?' He eased off, and Rose pulled free. 'Say you'll kill a sailor or two,' she told Mickey, squeezing his arm. 'It might keep those things back for a bit longer.'

He nodded bleakly and watched her run with Jay over to the cargo dump.

'Fingers crossed,' murmured Vida, and went to find herself a mutated sailor to threaten.

The store in the cargo dump was just as cold, wet and dark as Rose remembered. Dozens of freshly drowned people staggered round in the confined space, lost in a nightmare world of their own, wheezing for air. The rustle of the thick tarp overhead sounded like some great, scurrying animal was close by, and sent shivers through her.

She and Jay had scrambled on board the overland way. Were they expected? She didn't know. The water-things couldn't be too psychic, or they would have stopped them escaping. Maybe it was to do with the pheromone things – when the creatures used your head to send the apparitions, they could see inside your mind at the same time.

Maybe.

Whatever, she guessed they would know she was there soon enough.

'The flasks were kept over here,' said Jay, ducking through the dripping crowd to explore the shelved walls of the store. Rose could see better in the dark with these heightened, pearly eyes; there was a moonlit glow to everything she saw. 'Quite close to the edge of the split, but the crate was strapped down. So maybe…'

That word again. Rose was getting sick of possibilities. She wanted a good, hard, firm fact.

'Yes!' Jay hissed, crouching over something. 'Some must have fallen out, but the crate itself is sound. Give me a hand undoing these straps, then we can drag it out.'

'Come on, then.' But as Rose splashed across the floor to join him, the silent drowned stopped their dead march. 'Something I said?' she murmured, ducking between their heaving bodies until she reached the crate. The thick plastic straps bit into her prune-like skin as she scrabbled at them. *God, what I wouldn't do for some moisturiser.*

Then she heard a sucking noise behind her. Whirled around.

The ranks of the drowned had parted, to reveal three *things*. Glutinous and white, they were slithering over the wet floor towards her.

Rose's stomach turned. They looked to be part slug, part fish. Two long, needle-like tusks stuck out dangerously from the white jelly flesh of their faces.

'Jay,' she said shakily, backing away, 'we've been rumbled.'

He swore, tugged at the top of one of the flasks. 'Can we use these on them?'

'I don't know how they work,' Rose told him. 'What are we meant to do with them, anyway?'

'I dunno, I can't get it out of the crate!' Jay smashed his fist against the metal. 'Useless!'

'Uh-oh, here come more of them!' The pallid creatures were uncoiling from the dank darkness beneath the shelving, pushing out their heads like giant snails.

'These ones don't have a human body,' he reasoned, 'so they're slow.'

'They don't have to be fast,' Rose reminded him. 'They can control the water.'

'But they can't hurt us, can they? Not with what's inside us!'

'They won't have to! Just wash us back into the river, along with the latest recruits. Drag us back down into the pit.' She stared round helplessly. 'Back to square one.'

'Then we'll have to leg it while we can,' said Jay. He readied himself to jump the encroaching creatures. Then he stopped. 'Oh, no.'

A towering grey-brown wedge of solid Thames was paring away from the surface, ready to come crashing down on the cargo trailer.

The police, the soldiers, they couldn't cope any more. There were too many people crowding the street, pushing against the barriers. Keisha watched, grinding her teeth and feeling horribly helpless as the disaster waiting to happen finally lost all patience.

'Maybe we could turn this thing and block the street,' said Jackie. But there were cars packed solid all around the tanker now, the blare of horns adding to the shouting and the sirens. 'We can't just sit here.'

'Maybe…' Keisha closed her eyes. 'Maybe Rose was wrong.'

'You want to join that lot out there after what she said?'

'I don't know what to think any more.'

'Then I'll tell you.' She opened the door of the cab, let in more of the din and clamour. 'We've got to do *something* to try and stop this.'

'There's nothing we can do!' Keisha yelled. 'Don't go, Jackie, please. Everyone goes and leaves me. Jay, Mum –'

'Your mum could be out there now in that lot!'

'– and I can't… I can't do this…' Tears prickled behind her eyes. 'Please don't go.'

She reached out to be held. Just as Jackie was pulled from out of the cab by someone in the mob outside.

'No!' Keisha screamed. 'Get off her!' Before she even knew what she was doing she had scrambled over the seat and jumped down into the milling crowd. She shook the tears from her eyes, but Jackie was already lost from sight. And now two more men had seized control of the tanker. One of them slid into the driver's seat. A soldier's gun went off close by. The engine bit into life as if in reply. The tanker lurched forwards, shunting the sea of people on, starting a fresh panic. Keisha glimpsed Jackie now, caught up in the crush of bodies.

The soldiers fell back as the barriers broke and overturned. The desperate mob surged forwards towards the river, taking Jackie and Keisha with them.

* * *

Rose stared as the body of water loomed ever closer to the cargo dump, ready to burst over them with incredible force. 'Maybe they can't kill us,' she said, 'but they're gonna make sure they teach us a good lesson!'

The creatures had stopped their slithering advance, watching them, their huge dead-fish eyes still glinting with malice. The eyes of the drowned fixed on them too in silent recrimination. She looked away, looked down...

'The crate!' she yelled over the oncoming roar. 'Jay, grab hold of the crate!'

'It's no good, it's not heavy enough,' he told her. 'The wave will wash it out with us.'

'Exactly!' She hugged the crate, gripping on as hard as she could. 'If they're gonna take us, they can have this too.' Jay joined her, scrabbling for something to hold. 'Maybe we can find a way to use it, or –'

Then the wave struck with the force of a truck. The ground tipped and the freezing water sledge-hammered Rose's back, knocking all breath from her, engulfing everyone and everything in the store. She, Jay and the crate were sent smashing into one side. Grimly she clung on as they were swilled back out of the dump with a bundle of bodies and into the river. Were the white things coming too? She couldn't tell. Her vision was speckled with black and silver. Was Jay still holding on, or had he been washed clear somewhere? There were so many dark figures falling through the water alongside her it was impossible to tell. Gasping for breath, she found that the water tasted good in her lungs, wanted to be sick. There were voices shouting for her – Mickey's the loudest, and Vida's too – but she couldn't catch the words over the roaring in her temples.

The crate dragged her down but she wasn't going to let go now, not if this was the one thing the Doctor said could hurt these things.

She felt herself snatched by the dark currents of the river, shut her eyes and clung on as she was tugged down deeper and deeper.

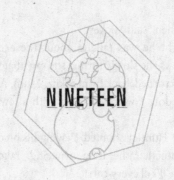

NINETEEN

'Rose!' Vida yelled from the river's stone edge as the girl was plucked back down beneath the water.

'It's no good,' said Mickey, staring in disbelief over the shoulder of the sailor he held in a necklock. 'She's gone.'

'And so have the tracers.' Vida hugged her own sailor dismally. 'That's it, then.'

Huntley shook his head. 'We can dive down and get them!'

Vida pointed down at the churning water. A thick, white shape undulated beneath the surface, like a giant slug. 'Into that?'

'I thought we *wanted* the tracers in the water?' said Mickey.

'The release trigger for the flasks is built into the bottom of the crate. Without that the contents are locked inside. Useless.'

Feeling numb, she barely looked up as a fresh wave of noise crashed across from the far bank of the river. A seething scrum of people had broken through the barriers. They jumped or fell screaming into the river, or surged over the boats still moored there to throw themselves in. Hundreds of them.

'That's it, then,' said Mickey.

She thought he was talking about the exodus into the Thames. But as she slowly turned she saw that the pirate and the kid had returned, back from asking Mum. And with them was Commodore Powers, together with a few other fright-night friends.

'Stay back!' Huntley shouted. Waving his bit of glass about, he looked pathetic rather than menacing. 'Take another step closer and we'll kill every carrier.'

Mickey produced the other hand grenade. 'And this'll make sure of it.'

But even if he'd meant it, he would never get the chance.

Too late, Vida saw the water pooling at their feet. A moment later, two more of the ravaged figures burst into being – a submarine captain and an old man in a greatcoat. In a blur of bloated flesh, Huntley's makeshift blade was smacked flying. The old man, pearl-eyes gleaming, pushed Mickey to the ground and grabbed Vida by the throat, while Powers led the others in a sudden, stumbling charge to get the rest of them.

'Get on with it, then,' the Doctor snarled. The queen had oozed round behind him, squelching and slithering, getting herself into position. Suddenly, the sinister fishermen released him, stood away. 'About time,' he said, 'I've lost all feeling in my arms waiting for –'

The sharp tips of her giant mandibles probed the back of his neck. It felt as if scalding hot water was pumping into his body.

'Feeling in the arms back now, thanks,' he gasped. Then it seemed he could do nothing but boil as the probes pushed into his spine.

Keisha wanted to scream but the breath had been all but crushed from her lungs by the packed crowds. She was being carried backwards on to the wharf, struck something solid. A metal pole, a sign warning you not to park here.

So fine me, thought Keisha.

Twisting round, she grabbed hold of the pole, clung to it against the tide of people. She could do this. She could hold on.

Then she glimpsed the girl being jostled towards her. Seven or eight, maybe, a black girl, wide-eyed and terrified. No one was with her or watching over her. She had been abandoned.

'Look out!' she yelled at the crowd. 'That little girl's gonna get trampled or...'

No one was listening. No one even looked, except the girl herself. Keisha stared all around desperately as the people shoved against her. Heard big splashes, explosions as people hit the river. Where were the soldiers now, or the police? Someone had to do something about the little girl. It couldn't be down to her. Not her.

There were so many shouts and screams all around her. But she could only hear one voice now, from hours and hours ago. Rose's voice.

'Sort your life out, Keisha. No one's gonna do it for you.'

The little girl was being swept past her, reaching out. Keisha just stared, paralysed. And by the time she'd reached out her own hand in response, it was too late. The girl had been bustled by.

'Stop!' Keisha screamed. And she let go of the pole, fell fighting into the crowd, to get to the girl before she was crushed or went over the edge.

Vida gasped as Mickey charged between her and the old man, breaking them apart. She staggered back to the river's edge, choking, as Mickey was clubbed to the ground. Powers and his friends had all but subdued Huntley and the others. On the far bank people were still cascading into the river like a human waterfall, and in desperation Vida was about to throw herself into the grey waters – when it bubbled up, right in front of her eyes.

The crate, tossed about on the river, with Rose still clinging on to it like a half-drowned rat.

'Wouldn't let me in,' Rose shouted frantically, filthy water pouring from her mouth. 'I think they know these things can hurt them. Want rid of them, but not of me –'

The water foamed white around Rose and then erupted, throwing her clear as the entire crate was literally spat out of the water. With a clanking crash it landed upside-down on the bank.

Vida stared at it disbelievingly for a few seconds. There it was, their one shot at somehow fighting back. But without the proper activation signal there was no way to release the tracers from the flasks. Unless...

The old man was scuttling towards her again.

Vida broke into a run, fell upon the crate, tried to heave it back towards the river. 'Mickey, that other grenade, where'd it go?' He was still lying on the ground. Was he knocked out, or worse? Panic and fear lent her strength and the crate budged a little way. She pushed again. 'Mickey, if we can just –'

But then the old man's hand clamped around her mouth, wormed into water that started to force its way down her throat.

Holding her breath, weeping with fear, Vida kept furiously shoving at the crate, nudging it back towards the river's edge – until the old man hauled her clear. He started to drag her away, arms and legs flailing...

Why had he stopped?

Vida looked down and saw that Rose had resurfaced and was gripping the old man firmly round the ankle, anchoring herself to him as something in the water tried to drag her back under.

The old man seemed to sink into the pavement as his lower body turned liquid to shake off Rose. But while he was distracted, with the last of her strength Vida twisted free, spluttering for breath, and stumbled back over to the crate. She strained to shift it but her head was spinning; she was too weak.

Then a hand clapped down on her shoulder.

It was Mickey. And in his other hand he had the grenade.

'Found it,' he said. 'Now what?'

'Help me with this.'

With both of them behind it, the crate scraped across the concrete till it sat teetering on the edge. Vida looked back. The old man was free once more, turning to face them.

'We've got to blow it apart once it's in the water,' she panted.

'Five-second fuse on these things,' said Mickey, trying to jam it into a split in the crate's casing. 'What about when it goes under? Will water put it out?'

'I don't know. Jam it in!'

But now the old man was hunched over them. He grabbed hold of Mickey with one hand and threw him into the river. But the grenade was still wedged in place. The drowned child ran towards Vida, grinning, water spilling from its ears and nose.

It threw itself on to her back. But Vida didn't let its cold, dead weight shift her. She depressed the safety handle, pulled on the pin.

5...

By some miracle, the grenade stayed in place. The child's hands scrabbled for her throat.

4...

Tendrils of water coiled round her throat like steel bands and squeezed.

3...

Her vision blurring, holding her breath, Vida pushed herself and the crate forwards into the water with a cold splash.

2...

At once she was steered away and down into the dark depths of the river, the child riding her like a jockey. But what about the crate? Would it be thrown straight back out again?

1...

The blackness grew absolute. *Please God, let it not all have been for nothing.*

Rose had used the last of her strength trying to stop the old man from getting Vida. Now she gave herself up to the darkness and the hungry current.

Then shockwaves blasted through the water. She was aware of a tang in her mouth, a cold chemical taste. Her mind fired up with the realisation.

And then Rose thought of the Doctor, shut her eyes as the entrance to the drainage channel loomed, ready to swallow her. *Will he ever know?* she wondered. *Will the Doctor know we did it?*

And then suddenly there he was. She could see him, eyes tight shut, standing up in some blinding white place. Standing in a bubbling pool of water with a monster close behind, its two needle-tusks inserted deep into his neck. He looked terrible, sweat literally pouring from his shocking-white skin, drenching his clothes. But somehow he must have sensed that her image was there, for his eyes opened Bambi-wide. She felt he could see her as clear and bright as the moon. And he forced a wonky smile.

'Of course you did it,' he said.

Sinking to his knees, he put his fingers to his temples, and shouted at the top of his lungs.

'Doctor!' Rose didn't see or hear what happened next, because she was back in the black water, sinking like a stone.

The Doctor felt like barbed wire was being dragged round his head, snagging on every nerve. A bright ball of light was searing through his senses. Slowly it became a vast eye, filling his mind, pearly and lolling in its encrusted carapace.

'Now your cells are ours, Doctor.' The eerie voice held no triumph, as if it had always known things would end this way. 'We have you.'

He spoke aloud, an anchor to the real world he could no longer see through his stinging eyes. 'Well, *actually*… I might just have *you*.'

'We are linked to you now. You are as one with the hive.'

'Yes, I am,' the Doctor agreed. Slowly he straightened, forcing himself to his feet. 'My mind is your mind, and all that.'

'We swim the same cold, deep water.'

'Sorry, old love, but I think you might be in *hot* water.' The Doctor gritted his teeth. 'Because I *let* you into my head. I needed you up close and personal so I could fathom your wavelength – puns fully intended, by the way. Because now I know that my friends have done what they set out to do, *I* can do *this*.'

In his mind he grabbed that heavy, dreadful eye and planted a big wet kiss upon it.

For a second he experienced life through the alien senses of the queen. The signals that teemed about her like life. The billions of scraps of information that fed her, that sped from her; that held the hive in harmony and allowed it to spread and grow.

He breathed in those senses. He experienced the hive dreaming through her, the first stirrings of life in every egg. And as he shuddered, so they stilled.

Quickly he felt out through the black complexity of the alien water and grasped the new filaments that were drifting out in clusters. All those tiny, transmitting filaments. Rose and Vida and Mickey and everyone had risked their lives to get them there.

And before the last of his strength could leave him he thought *over* the queen. He switched on those transmitters with a single murmured command. And he felt the same sting that she did as the water became alive with new signals.

The signatures were wrong, the wavelengths jarring and alien.

The harmony of the hive was shattered by a sea of dead static.

'How long have you prospered by poisoning love and longing?' the Doctor gasped. 'How many races have you tricked, drowned and slaughtered just so you can go on existing? Well, it stops here.' A piercing shriek jolted through his mind but he did not falter. 'That's not just feedback. It's *pay*back.'

The queen screamed and the Doctor screamed with her, cast out into the deeps and the blackness.

Jackie was down in the water with so many others, trying to swim back to the bank. Her limbs were cramping up. People kept on piling into the water. Some were already swimming with determination for the far side of the river; others flailed about, screaming for help that would never come as the bodies rained down.

She glimpsed Keisha, her lovely hair wet and plastered over

her face so she couldn't see, straining to hold a little black girl above her head, out of the water.

Then something grabbed hold of Jackie's leg, tugged her down before she could catch a breath.

Amid the thrashing legs and arms of the frantic swimmers, fat white creatures were circling. Jackie caught the dead glint of their eyes in the murk. She couldn't free herself, flailing and floundering as she was dragged ever deeper down.

Then the water around her seemed to convulse, to bubble and froth with a life of its own. The white things fell away from her, and she was being propelled upwards, shooting out from the freezing water like a cork from a champagne bottle.

Surviving the blast in the water had been the easy bit. The child had drained away but Vida was still caught in the eddying current, drawing every last smack of oxygen from what must surely be her last breath. She shut her eyes as the creatures swarmed around her, pricked her with spindly tusks, tore at her skin as if they wanted to tear her apart in revenge for what she had done.

She felt herself spinning helplessly. A whirlpool must have sprung up. Now it was sucking her in.

Or pushing her out.

In a dizzying rush she broke the surface of the water, along with one or two of the laws of physics.

Somehow she stayed floating there, lying on her back, whooping down breaths of smoky London air. It was sweet as a flower's perfume. What the hell was happening? Instinctively she made to start swimming, but the water didn't want to know. She couldn't force her legs or arms beneath it. It was as if she was rolling on the most comfortable bed in creation. On the far side of the river, she saw many others in the same bizarre yet quite agreeable predicament.

Close beside her, Mickey popped up, cut and bruised and bewildered. 'What's going on?' he spluttered. 'Where did those things go?'

Vida looked. Outside Stanchion House, the grisly, bloated figures of the long-since drowned had vanished, leaving Huntley and the sailors in a daze on the concrete concourse. 'I don't know,' she said, waving at Huntley, who was getting groggily to his feet. 'I don't have a clue.'

Back on the far bank, the people still tumbling into the Thames were bouncing back up, shrieking and screaming and splashing, but otherwise unharmed. There was no current, so they didn't drift. And all across the water, as far as the eye could see, heads were bobbing into view, strange pearls given up by the river bed.

Vida was so gobsmacked she let in a mouthful of the water – then spat it out and grimaced. 'Salt! This river's awash with salt!'

Mickey managed to balance himself in a kneeling position. 'Normal salt or weird alien salt?'

'Give you two guesses,' she offered. 'But that's why we're floating! We can't sink!' She gingerly stood up. 'Look! I'm walking on water!'

But Mickey wasn't looking. He was pointing past her, laughing and cheering because the stodgy river had parted to allow Rose through as well, close to the bank outside

Stanchion House. She lay still on her back for a few moments, and Vida's face fell.

But then Rose jerked up, her hands flying to her face.

'You all right?' Mickey bellowed, scrambling across the water to reach her.

Rose didn't answer. Vida walked unsteadily across to join them. It was like treading the skin on a tapioca pudding.

'Are you all right?' Mickey asked again, more softly.

'I think so.' Her fingers traced the thin scars that lined her cheeks and neck. 'These gill things… It's like they're healing.'

'Mine too,' Huntley said incredulously. Vida saw tears well in his eyes, and saw also that they were blue. The silvery tinge had left them. 'Tissue regeneration. But it's so fast…' He hugged the nearest sailor, whose face was still grisly, like those of his crewmates. They had been subjected to the creatures' influence for longer, but the fact they were doing better than Commodore Powers had to be a good sign. The commodore's body lay in a puddle like a discarded bag of skin and uniform, slowly dissolving. Of the other monsters – the old man, the pirate, the woman in the dress – there was no trace at all beyond a pool of evil-smelling water.

Mickey stared at Rose, at Huntley, round at the people spewed up by the salty river and walking on water. The bemused smile on his face slowly grew. 'What happened? What the hell happened?'

'What d'you think happened?' Rose yelled, a grin breaking open her face. 'The *Doctor* happened!'

'Oi. Less of the past tense,' came a weary but very familiar voice.

'Doctor!' Rose led the chorus, just as she led the way over to grab him in a hug.

'Whoa! Steady, steady.' He gently disengaged himself, and now Vida noticed the dark bruising beneath his eyes. 'I've just been tangling with a dirty great queen in an underground dungeon.' He clapped Huntley on the back, leaned in conspiratorially. 'Shame I didn't think ahead. In this part of town I could have sold tickets.'

TWENTY

'Come on, then,' Vida demanded. 'How did you do it? What *did* you do?'

'It's not all down to me,' said the Doctor curtly. Then he offered a crooked smile. 'Thanks to you lot, I was able to set those little chemical transmitters going. Swamped the hive's means of communication. Without information, without co-ordination, the group mind was shattered. They went to pieces.'

'But how come I'm healing up already?' Rose was still stroking her cheeks, and Vida saw that scores more people were doing the same while they wobbled about on the skin of the water. 'My eyes feel normal again. Do they look normal?'

'Gorgeous,' he agreed cheerily. 'The genetic damage was being enforced by the hive mind – alien proteins and mental power, combining to turn you into a suitable host for growing the eggs.' The Doctor cupped her cheek. 'And now the mind's fallen apart, so the damage will be undone. Even the dead eggs should dissolve to nothing.'

'So what's happened to those fish creatures?' Vida asked.

'You've been paddling in them,' he said casually. 'I told you, they went to pieces. Their DNA has unravelled. And unless I'm very much mistaken, the proteins they manipulated have been broken down into salts.' He jumped clumsily on to the surface of the Thames, dipped his finger and licked it. 'I'm *not* very much mistaken,' he announced, grimacing.

'I never doubted it for a second,' said Vida, relief sweeping over her. 'So it's over?'

He paused for a while, swaying, not quite himself. 'We're getting there,' he said at length, and then he nodded. Just the once.

'Where's Jay?' asked Rose, looking round anxiously. 'I lost him when those things were trying to drown us all over again. And Mum and Keish…' Her face clouded. 'I tried to turn them back, but what if they fell in?'

The Doctor gestured round the river. 'The drowned are bouncing back, as you can see. Human DNA completely regenerates itself every couple of months, though the mental scars might not fade as quickly. Vida, perhaps you could call Vice Admiral Kelper at Aldgate and make sure he does something about that once he's fished everyone out of the water…'

'Will the Thames ever get back to normal?' Mickey wondered.

'Does it matter? I quite like it this way. Less congestion. Could be a big draw for the tourists too.' The Doctor frowned. 'Fish might be less keen, though. So it's probably just as well these new salts will dissolve over time.' He nodded thoughtfully. 'I like fish.'

'With chips in newspaper,' Rose teased him.

'We'll be able to monitor the spread of the pollutants,' said Vida. 'We'll make sure there's nothing left, Andrew and I. Can we go and find him?'

'There'll be a lot of people down there in need of someone to talk to,' said Huntley thoughtfully.

Vida frowned. 'Can't be many counsellors who specialise in post-alien mutation.'

'*Yellow Pages* is full of them,' the Doctor assured her. 'You'll cope.'

'You know, I think I probably will,' she said casually, enjoying the feel of the afternoon sun on her wet skin.

As if she dealt with stuff like this every day.

Keisha sat on the wharf, wrapped in a tin-foil blanket and sipping Red Cross tea, hoping that the police had found the little girl's parents by now. They had cordoned off this part of the bank and no one seemed keen to break that barrier on either side. When the sailors emerged from the river with their shiny eyes and slits in their faces, the authorities tried to hide them from view. But Keisha had caught sight of Jay through the confusion of the crowd and she'd struggled, threatened and beaten her way through to get to him. His eyes were messed up but they were real tears he cried as he held her.

Now she rested her head on his shoulder as they stared out over the unlikely scenes of fear and jubilation on the solid grey stripe of the Thames.

'Mum came down,' she said. 'She called me. She was

coming to see me and we were gonna go to you together. Something must have happened, I guess.'

He nodded.

'But when all this calms down… when you're feeling better again, Jay…' She looked at him. 'Well, we'll find her.'

'Maybe.'

'She came all that way, Jay. She ain't forgotten us.'

'She only came 'cause I made her, Keish. Like I made you.' He snorted softly. 'Finally, I could make people come back, just by wishing. And like a wish, it wasn't real.'

'But you don't know. Maybe when she sees us again –'

'You can't build a better future by keeping hold of the past.' He took her hand. 'Mum ain't coming back, sis, wherever she is, whatever she said.'

Keisha didn't speak for a while. 'When she called up the flat out of the blue… I was going crazy thanks to you, and it was such a shock, it sort of made me snap out of it. I guess that if she'd never gone away…'

'Well, maybe we've got something to thank her for after all, then,' said Jay.

They looked at each other and, after a few seconds, shook their heads. 'Nah.'

Jay laughed, held Keisha closer. 'Things can never be the way they were, 'cause we're none of us the *people* we were.' He smiled ruefully, waved at his eyes. 'Or did you notice that?'

A tear teased itself down her cheek. 'Stop it,' she said, and found she was talking to herself as much as to Jay. 'You'll get better. You'll get back to how you were.'

'I'm hoping I'll become more than that, if I try.' He paused.

'Like Rose. No matter what happened, or how bad things got… she never stopped trying. You know?'

Keisha nodded. 'She's so different to how she was. She's… amazing.'

'What about you?' Jay prodded her. 'You probably saved that little girl's life, sis. You made a difference.'

'I didn't think. Just blundered in as usual.'

'That's all life is. Blundering about from one thing to the next.'

Keisha half-smiled. 'And hoping for the best, yeah?'

'Gotta keep hoping. 'Cause things keep changing.' He put his arm round her again. 'And if we want to, we can change with them.'

The Doctor was all for clearing off as soon as possible, as usual. But Rose wasn't going anywhere till she knew the people she loved were safe. Luckily – for her nerves and his attention span – the news came sooner rather than later.

They were down in the gigantic labs, helping the baffled, frightened victims of the waterhive out of the drainage pit and the darkness. It had been a bit of a scramble but everyone got out alive, Anne and PC Fraser included. Vida had found her boss and the two had enjoyed a tearful reunion that bordered on the indecent.

'Good working relationship,' Rose observed.

Mickey looked at her shyly. 'Proper hug sounds good after all this.'

'Does it?' She glanced round to check on the Doctor. He was standing alone in the wrecked laboratory, his back to them all. 'Well, Professor Huntley's got a good grip. Try him.'

'Funny.'

'I mean it!'

Huntley was moving between bedraggled groups of survivors, giving the plainest explanations he could manage and trying to help. 'I've never met so many people in my life,' he said, all puffed up and proud.

'Plenty more where they came from above ground,' said Vida, leading Andrew over by the hand. He looked to be in a bit of a daze, but Rose saw his scars were healing even faster than her own. 'Now I'd better get this one to a hospital and catch up with Kelper. There's a hell of a mess to clean up.'

'Lucky he's got that cleaner with him,' said Mickey.

'You joke, but he's already roped in her *and* Jodie. They've set up a special emergency clinic at Aldgate station – anyone who's come into contact with the water needs to register for a special jab. That way the navy can keep a quiet eye on everyone who's been in the water, just to check there are no long-term effects.'

Rose nodded. The Doctor didn't seem to think there would be, but better safe than sorry.

'Will you and the Doctor be sticking around?' Vida asked her.

She wrinkled her nose. 'Not really our style.'

'Uh-huh. Well, I won't ask where you'll be going…'

'We don't even know ourselves!'

'But wherever it is – don't drink the water.' She smiled, blew Rose and Mickey a kiss and walked away, Andrew trailing behind her.

'You don't have to go yet, do you?' Mickey said.

Rose didn't answer.

Mickey took a step closer. 'Nothing happened with Keisha,' he said.

She looked away. 'It's all right. It was all ages ago, anyway.'

'I mean it. Stay and you can ask her!'

'I don't need to ask her.'

'Nothing went on! I was so cut up about you going that –'

'Good choice of words, cut up,' she said, touching her scars. 'Like it.'

'Will you just listen?'

'Honest, Mickey, it's all right.' She half-smiled. 'Today I was drowned and turned into a fish. Sort of puts things in perspective a bit.'

Mickey shook his head sadly. 'So even the bad stuff that happens when the Doctor's around wins out over you and me?'

She put a hand on his chest. 'I believe you, OK? And I'm sorry for what I put everybody through. How it changed everything so fast. You and me, we were different people then. And though we'll go on changing…'

He nodded. 'Maybe some things can stay the same.'

His arms were just slipping round her for a close hug when her mobile started to trill, despite the total soaking it had received. That was the Doctor's jiggery-pokery for you. Just as well, since with all that tampering, the warranty must be royally stuffed.

'Some things will *always* stay the same,' groaned Mickey. 'That'll be your mum!' And he was right of course.

She was calling from a box. 'You all right, sweetheart? I've been queuing for this phone for an hour. An hour! We've been so worried, Rose, me and Keisha. You've been driving us out of our minds, you have. So *are* you all right?'

'I'm fine,' Rose insisted, 'so's Mickey. So's himself.' *I think.* The Doctor was still standing well apart from the others. 'What about you, Mum, you OK? Where are you?'

'Down the embankment. We've got the Red Cross, Sally Army, coppers taking our names. It's crazy. Oh, and I met this *gorgeous* man on the river! Most people were in a bit of a daze, but me and him, we were so excited we ended up dancing this fandango, right across the Thames! He's a lovely mover –'

'Is Keish all right?' she interrupted. 'Is she there?'

'She's with Jay. They're catching up. But you wouldn't believe the state of him.'

Oh, yes, I would. 'He helped save us, Mum. He was brilliant.'

'Well, the navy doctors will be getting to him soon,' Jackie went on. 'They'll look after their own, won't they? Oh, hang on, I've run out of change. These things eat money! Will I see you, sweetheart? See you soon, I mean?'

The phone clicked as she was disconnected.

'Yeah, Mum,' Rose whispered. 'See you soon.'

She switched off her mobile and glanced over at the Doctor. He was facing her now. Sneakers wet through, suit dishevelled, hair all over the place.

Smiling. It was time to go.

She looked back at Mickey. 'I'll be back again. In about ten minutes, probably. Just you wait.'

And though neither of them really believed it, they smiled

and nodded as if it was true. She pressed a kiss against his bruised cheek, waved to Vida, Huntley and the others. Then turned and walked slowly away, texting Keisha as she went.

Wotever you do b happy. C u soon. Love rxxx

She reached the Doctor and he raised his eyebrows at her. 'Finished?'

'Not quite.'

PS Big hugs to your gorgeous bruv

She pressed send and then switched off the phone. 'You know, there was this bloke who used to scare me and Keisha when we were kids. Old Scary we called him. He used to go around shouting stuff in this horrible voice, all sorts of things. He even made the nice bits sound frightening. I'd hear him from my room sometimes. I'd hide under the covers and listen to him going on all night.' She cast back her mind. '"Many waters cannot quench love." That was one he came out with a lot. "Neither can the floods drown it."'

'And?'

Rose shrugged. 'Maybe he wasn't really so scary after all.'

'You want scary?' The Doctor took her hand. 'I'll show you scary. On the planet Jacdusta in the Dustijek nebula, the chips cost a tenner a portion! And they don't even come wrapped in newspaper…'

Together they walked away.

New adventures were waiting.

Acknowledgements

Special thanks go to all those who helped with the *Feast* when their plates were already full. To Russell T Davies for his input on the early storylines, and to Helen Raynor for always smiling when she must have felt like tearing her long Welsh hair out. To Denis Dallaire for sage advice on how rear and vice admirals would converse. And to Justin Richards for inviting Jac and me to the party once again; his astute edits have improved this book no end.

About the Author

Stephen Cole used to edit magazines and books, and in the late 1990s looked after the BBC's range of *Doctor Who* novels, videos and audio adventures. Now he spends his time writing, chiefly books for children of all ages.

Recent projects include *Thieves Like Us* (a spooky action-adventure novel for young adults), the ongoing fantasy series *Astrosaurs* for younger children, and the surreal school mystery series *One Weird Day at Freekham High*. He lives in front of a computer in Buckinghamshire, venturing out of his office now and then to find his wife, Jill, and young son, Tobey.

DOCTOR·WHO

Monsters and Villains

By Justin Richards

ISBN 0 563 48632 5
UK £7.99 US $12.99/$15.99 CDN

For over forty years, the Doctor has battled against the most dangerous monsters and villains in the universe. This book brings together the best – or rather the worst – of his enemies.

Discover why the Daleks were so deadly; how the Yeti invaded London; the secret of the Loch Ness Monster; and how the Cybermen have survived. Learn who the Master was, and – above all – how the Doctor defeated them all.

Whether you read it on or behind the sofa, this book provides a wealth of information about the monsters and villains that have made *Doctor Who* the tremendous success it has been over the years, and the galactic phenomenon that it is today.

The Stone Rose

By Jacqueline Rayner

ISBN 0 563 48643 0

UK £6.99 US $11.99/$14.99 CDN

Mickey is startled to find a statue of Rose in a museum – a statue that is 2,000 years old. The Doctor realises that this means the TARDIS will shortly take them to ancient Rome, but when it does, he and Rose soon have more on their minds than sculpture.

While the Doctor searches for a missing boy, Rose befriends a girl who claims to know the future – a girl whose predictions are surprisingly accurate. But then the Doctor stumbles on the hideous truth behind the statue of Rose – and Rose herself learns that you have to be very careful what you wish for…

The Resurrection Casket

By Justin Richards

ISBN 0 563 48642 2

UK £6.99 US $11.99/$14.99 CDN

Starfall – a world on the edge, where crooks and smugglers hide in the gloomy shadows and modern technology refuses to work. And that includes the TARDIS.

The pioneers who used to be drawn by the hope of making a fortune from the mines can find easier picking elsewhere. But they still come – for the romance of it, or in the hope of finding the lost treasure of Hamlek Glint – scourge of the spaceways, privateer, adventurer, bandit…

Will the TARDIS ever work again? Is Glint's lost treasure waiting to be found? And does the fabled Resurrection Casket – the key to eternal life – really exist? With the help of new friends, and facing terrifying new enemies, the Doctor and Rose aim to find out…